The Pretender

Also by Andrew Fisher

Smoke Ring Day

Mandatory Eight Count

THE PRETENDER (1973–1976)

Andrew Fisher

International Psychoanalytic Books (IPBooks)
New York • IPBooks.net

Published by IPBooks, Queens, NY
Online at: www.IPBooks.net

ISBN 978-1-969031-08-3

Contents

To Lyndy, my constant devoted presence,
whose loving eye helped navigate the ship to shore.

CHAPTER 1

Life Goes On (Fall 1973)

Carole's dead. Killed in a freak car accident. Now what? If there is a what. Is there a what? Have to head to Cleveland where I will attend her funeral. Just a basket case. So bereft. Can I get up off the canvas? Do I even want to? A big part of me says no. Why bother? She's gone, so what is left for me to live for? I loved her so deeply and fully. I see only darkness in front of me. Earl, Rosmary, and Steve, my housemates, who I hardly know, are sweet and sympathetic. But they have their own lives. I will not go back to therapy. I will not. I will find a way on my own this time. If I find my way back at all.

For the time being, I tried to function. First things first. I called Rose Lane, the Quarterway house, and talked to Hal, my buddy who also worked there, who did minimal advocating. He didn't really need to. They all liked me there. The powers that be saw that I had unusual rapport and empathy with the residents, who, after all, were just like me. Former psych patients. Except they were in a Quarterway house, three quarters of the way back towards independence, whereas I was all the way through. They told me they wanted me to come back when I was ready, and granted me a leave of absence, a kind of temporary disability, so I would qualify for unemployment insurance when I returned from Cleveland.

My trip to Cleveland, where Carole's parents lived, was a shit show. Carole's abrasive, abusive mother. Her alcoholic, sweet, passive father. I was barely acknowledged by her mother. Carole's father, Don, tried to be nice, but he was in mourning. She was their only child after all. It was inconceivable to me that they were not aware that Carole and I had been living together for more than two years. They knew we were a couple, but not "living in sin." Either that, or they just didn't want to know. Parents could be like that. I got in, got out. Luckily, Paul and John, two of my old Columbus OSU friends, not former Beatles but also friends of Carole's, made the trek up from Columbus to say their goodbyes and offer me moral and emotional support. It helped. I was determined to carry on as the funeral brought to the fore who Carole was and what Carole would have wanted for me. Carry on, have your best life and that can be my legacy for you. That was my sense and what I gleaned. A very unselfish person to the core. So with a heavy heart, my inappropriate paean to LBJ, I said my ritualized goodbye to Carole and tried to get on with it.

I knew this was only the beginning of my grief and mourning. I wasn't that stupid. But by the time I got back to Berkeley, with unemployment money starting to come in and with some cash from my dad to ease my move to California, I decided I needed a major change of pace and scenery. Maybe Reno, to clear my head. Why Reno? Gambling and sex.

CHAPTER 2

Reno (October 10, 1973)

I had enough dough from my unemployment insurance from my job as night watchman and staff counselor, along with the remainder of Dad's gift from when I left Ohio, to come to California, my reward for all of the success I had in the previous two years. Success included doing well in school, having a successful relationship with Carole, and most importantly, developing and maintaining some emotional stability. That was his major way of saying he was proud of me, and I didn't say no. I liked the dough. In the words of the Humphrey Bogart character, Fred C. Dobbs, in the movie *The Treasure of the Sierra Madre*, "I need dough and plenty of it." So after paying for rent, food and the essentials after Ohio now going on two months, I still had about $500 to play with. I headed up to Reno, taking $200 to try my hand at the craps table.

The drive took about four hours, getting more and more beautiful as I drove into the Sierra foothills around Auburn. Arriving in Reno around dusk, I quickly parked my car on State Street, Reno's main gambling thoroughfare, and raced into Harrah's, the big hotel on the strip, and found a $1 craps table. I surveyed the scene from outside the circle of players for a few minutes, and then, eager to play, as was my wont, plunked my initial $1 bet down on the pass line. I lost. And I kept losing. After only fifteen minutes, I was down $160. Across the table, I noticed a tall, chunky, forty-something gentleman with a longish gray beard eyeballing me. Finally, he walked over to where I was standing and said, "You're out of line. You're playing a Martindale, which is a sure loser."

He then proceeded to explain to me what a Martindale was. It was a betting system, where if you lose an initial bet of, say, one dollar, you doubled your bet on the next throw to make up for your initial loss. If you ran a streak of six or seven losses in a row, you could be betting $128 to win back your initial $1 investment. Not a good system.

After this spiel about the Martindale, the man introduced himself. His name was Bill Johnson. He told me that he had a system called the "System of Averaging Down," which he could teach me.

By this time I was tapped out, having blown the entire $200, minus ten bucks I kept for an emergency. I told him I was intrigued, but I would need to head back to Berkeley to get the rest of my dough, and I would meet him at the same spot, at 8pm the next night. Bill agreed, nodding his head. He told me one other thing.

He said, " I can teach you this craps system which works, this system of averaging down, but you need to know this. To be a success at gambling is to be a failure at life." Completely disregarding the spiritual bromide, but sort of intrigued, I said, "I'll be back tomorrow."

I drove home to Berkeley that night with my $10. Eager with anticipation, I got another $200 in cash from the bank the next day and drove back to Reno to meet Johnson at the designated spot. Johnson showed up right on time. A good sign. Johnson was a former used car salesman, divorced and straight, who had essentially dropped out of society to be a full-time gambler. Johnson taught me the ropes. This system of averaging down was a very conservative system where the lowest bet was 1/200 of your stake. It was designed to guarantee that you always bet very conservatively. If you won, you raised your bet only after you won at that level two out of three times. Likewise, if you lost, you went back one step to your previous level. All of this was structured to ensure that you never got "tapped out." In this system, if you exercised discipline, patience, and stamina, you could win a decent amount. I started the week with $200, and after forty hours of play, I doubled my money. But it was weird. It became a job. Bill and I slept in our cars through the day to save money. We also took advantage of 2-for-1 meal tickets at various casino restaurants. We gambled at night, but only with the craps dealers who were poor counters. The ones who might make an error in the bettor's favor when doling out the winnings. Johnson also had a method for throwing the dice. He would hold the dice flush when he wanted to make a seven or eleven (craps), and hold the dice at the edges and knuckle when he wanted to make a point (4,5,6,8,9,10). It seemed to work, strange as this may seem.

Bill and I did this for a month. Living like monks. Very austere. We'd gamble during the week, and drive back to Berkeley on weekends, where I put him up at my place. This, of course, was the opposite of what most people did, which was work during the week and gamble on weekends. But Bill and I saw ourselves as professionals. Disciplined, methodical, and scientific. Bill was a weird guy. His rap alternated between his gambling theories and methods, and recitations from this spiritual mentor of his, an Indian teacher named J. Krishnamurti who had rejected guru status, but had a sizable following nonetheless. He got me reading the guy and I must say, I got fascinated by him. It's where Johnson came up with the slogan, "To be a success at gambling is to be a failure at life." After a month, I was a success at gambling. Up $500. But I'd put in one hundred sixty hours, which averaged out to around $3.20 an hour, slightly above minimum wage. I guess you could say technically, I was a success. But it didn't feel like it. All the month had done was provide a diversion from my pain and suffering. A distraction. But now this diversion had become so monotonous, boring, and stultifying, that the diversion was more miserable than the original thing I was trying to escape. Almost.

The casino environment was really toxic. Cigarette smoke pervaded the place. Girls serving booze in their skimpy skirts, tits hanging out, designed to distract the gamblers. Free booze. The occasional ambulance for victims of heart attacks disrupted the festivities. The place reeked of high stress and desperation. Besides the street people who I befriended, people who Bill, a seasoned veteran of living off the casinos and streets, knew fairly well, and who I discovered firsthand were people just like people anywhere, except less pretentious, and in some ways, more interesting than your run-of-the-mill Joe, the environment overall was deadening.

There had to be a better way to distract myself. I found a little of it while up in the beautiful hills outside Reno. Bill and I frequently trekked, hiking to magnificent vistas while Bill lectured on healthful eating, spiritual living, and the moral failures of the gambling life. His hectoring and contradictory tone got old.

There was one other diversion, Mustang Ranch, the famous whorehouse in Sparks, Nevada, where prostitution was legal. I made a foray there one night by myself. Johnson wasn't into that kind of thing. He seemed kind of asexual. There, I discovered the "candy store." Girls would come out and line up, scantily clad, and the customer, instead of picking out a Snickers or a Milky Way bar, would pick an enticing female. I picked a blonde with sizable breasts.

She was nice enough. Professional, but aloof. The sex was perfunctory, mechanical. But at least it was sex. Barely.

After a month of Reno and its delights, I was done with gambling and prostitution. Johnson bid me adieu following another weekend in Berkeley. I never saw nor heard from him again. Now it was back to me. What would I do? How would I cope? How would I live?

CHAPTER 3

Ricky Returns (Early November, 1973)

It wouldn't take long before another distraction headed my way. This time, in the form of Ricky Sidelman, my oldest New Rochelle friend and tennis rival. Ricky called me up a few days after I decided not to return to Reno. He was in desperate straits. "Twisting" is the word he used. As in twisting in the wind. An apt phrase if there ever was one. Seems he'd been in Hawaii, Maui to be exact, a year out of Harvard, in an exploratory mode like the rest of us twenty-three-year-olds, living with a Harvard buddy, and experiencing a series of panic attacks that left him depressed, and very down on himself. When we reconnected, he was staying with a friend in San Francisco, another Harvard buddy attending UCSF medical school. When we spoke, he sounded awful. I came into San Francisco and we met up at his apartment near UCSF, in the outer Haight. Ricky, who had been an excellent tennis player, jogger, and health nut, was now smoking three packs a day and drinking heavily. He was a nervous wreck. He punctuated his distress by periodically ending his sentences with "kill me lord." He wasn't suicidal, just super anxious and very down on himself. Pretty miserable. The only thing not gone was his self-deprecatory sense of humor, which now was getting overtime duty due to his miserable mental state. I had never seen him like this in my whole life, and Ricky was my oldest friend, since second grade out on the Davis Elementary school baseball diamond, where we had met fifteen years earlier, in 1958.

From the start, Ricky and I clicked. He was one of the best baseball players amongst the eight-year-olds, as was I. But even more importantly, Ricky and I shared a preternaturally intense love for music. Rock music. We began purchasing 45s. My first was Frankie Avalon's "Dede Dinah." Rather laughable in retrospect. Ricky's was The Platters' "Great Pretender." We hung out a lot and had deep conversations about the planets and infinity and periodically, about classic kid's books. Ricky and I would peruse my father's old books, all of which were lodged in our basement bedroom's built in bookshelves. This library from my father's youth became like a treasure hunt for Ricky and me. Here, we found old, yellowing copies of "Treasure Island," "The Three Musketeers," Hawthorne's "House of the Seven Gables," and even "The Count of Monte Cristo." With each discovery, Ricky would let out a high-pitched scream, as if he had discovered buried treasure. The aged, crinkled, brown stained pages only added to the books' exoticism. By age eleven, both Ricky and I, avid readers, had gone through many of these children's classics, or at least the Classic Comics versions, enabling us to be able to wax eloquent.

As well as we got along, Ricky and I were rabid competitors on the baseball diamond, football field, and later, the tennis court, where we were about even, until, at the age of fourteen, Ricky went to a tennis camp. After that, he got good. Like seriously good. So good that he became the #1 singles player on the high school tennis team, and eventually, so good that he earned #1 in the East Coast 18-and-under rankings. As good as he was, he fell slightly below the professional level. He played in the National 18-and-under junior tennis championships, and went up against Roscoe Tanner, who would later be in the world top 10 for a few years. In their first-round match, Tanner's 140 mph serve proved too much, and Ricky succumbed 6-0, 6-2, which ended Ricky's professional aspirations just like that. Losing to Tanner that decisively made Ricky realize he had hit his limit, maxed out as a tennis player. And so Rick basically abandoned that ambition.

When Rick went to Harvard, he backed off the tennis and focused on his burgeoning singer-songwriting rock band career. Following in the vein of Van Morrison and John Fogarty, he began writing songs and playing in bands. From 9th grade until college, he played in a local band, first called the Breakers, and later The Valhalla Chemists. Rick sang and played rhythm guitar. That band was good enough, or maybe shrewd enough, to get invited to the Johnny Carson Tonight show. Ricky was focused and successful. I envied him, but not so much that it affected our relationship. He was focused and ambitious. And I was too intermittently motivated and focused to succeed at any one endeavor. Also, my history with myriad psychological problems had sidetracked me on numerous occasions, and for long periods of time. But now, with my grief from Carole's sudden death, and my determination to keep it together, and Ricky's out of nowhere panic attacks and resulting depression, in some ways we were on the same page again. Both struggling. But somehow, because of my history with mental problems, I knew the ropes and was less frightened by craziness. Ricky was clearly more bewildered and upset by his difficulties, and would frequently obsess and ruminate, which made things worse. Additionally, my efforts to bring out the source of his difficulties were blocked with evasions.

"What do you think was making you feel so scared back in Hawaii?" I would query.

"I don't know man. It's like too weird. I don't know. It's hard to talk about. Too strange. I don't know man."

In other words, my efforts got me nowhere, and left me feeling frustrated. Clearly, my buddy wanted nothing to do with uncomfortable feelings, so I gave up trying after several fruitless attempts. It was in these endeavors that I saw how different he and I were. I was more in touch with my feelings for better or worse, while Rick ran around his. Regardless, the two of us were quite a pair, and spent lots of time together, more than we had since we were little kids.

Ricky had majored in Social Relations at Harvard, a hybrid major combining psychology, sociology, and anthropology, and towards his senior year, specialized in a somewhat obscure psychoanalytical theory: Object Relations. Rick read all kinds of stuff in this area, and it served, at least in an intellectual sense, as an orienter for Rick, and as I became more familiar with the concepts, for myself as well. Harry Guntrip, one of the object relations theorists, a British analyst, was one of Ricky's favorites, and his concept of the "regressed ego" became one of our favorite pieces of jargon to bandy about to describe our various emotional states. It helped a little.

I would come to San Francisco frequently to visit Ricky, along with his roommate John, and John's girlfriend Lucy. Ricky had no car, so when he came to see me in Berkeley, he would take the BART over, or I would pick him up in my trusty Red Octopus, a Toyota Corona.

In addition to Ricky, I was getting friendlier with my housemates Earl, Rosmary, and Steve. I also had my OSU buddies, Hal (also from Rose Lane), Cal, another oval friend, the green area where I had met Hal at the same time, and a new guy named Doug who lived in Cal's apartment complex, where I'd spent a night or two before getting my own place. Doug and I gravitated to each other in particular, as we shared similar musical tastes, smoked pot, particularly when listening to music, and shared a mutual desire not to work. Like me, Doug was unemployed at this point, and also a quarter shy of graduating from OSU. He would also be going back to Cal-Berkeley to finish up his last quarter.

In another stroke of luck, I ran into Johnny Terner, a New Rochelle buddy who I had known in my Madison, Wisconsin depression days. He was also living in Berkeley now, obviously a popular place for us counterculture types. He turned me on to a regular weekend softball game on the UC campus at the girls' softball field, Barrows Field. There, I would meet my third set of friends.

CHAPTER 4

Dewey Softball

That day, a typical 70-degree sunny day in mid-November, I showed up at the usual 11 a.m. start time. A guy in his late twenties, with sideburns, medium-length hair, and a slight limp, approached me. His name was Dewey. He introduced himself, invited me to play, and explained that the first twenty people to show up played. "Choose up," we used to call it back home. Soon, other regulars appeared. There was Sol, the guy Terner had mentioned, a sociology grad student at Berkeley in his late twenties who played shortstop, who, it turned out, would be quite skilled in the field and adroit as a lead off singles hitter. Donn, a cofounder of the game with Dewey, was just back from traveling around the world. He was a bit older than the rest of us, thirty-two to be exact, and a union organizer. Liberal, not radical, an important distinction in Berkeley. David had a thick New York accent, and a quick wit, and everyone called him Statman. He was a man so obsessed with playing ball that he had kept weekly, monthly and yearly stats on every game, every player and every at bat for the last three years. Stat had the best pot, and a prodigious knowledge of sports, film and all kinds of music, the things I was obsessed with as well. We became fast friends. Hanging out with him was almost like being with my Bizarro World twin, for the Superman comic fans out there, as we would often refer to our connection.

The games were great. Fast pitch. Windmill style. The pitchers were very competent, delivering multiple kinds of pitches, and the games very competitive, with a fair amount of trash talking, but no fighting. After all, a lot of us were middle class Jewish guys, and fighting was not part of our modus operandi. Verbal abuse, yes. Throwing punches, no. Still, there were a couple of loose screws. Two army vets. Holden, in his late 30's, and a Korean war vet, barrel chested, was a very solid line drive hitter and decent fielder, but prone to making violent pronouncements, and booking in with an IQ in the low 80s at most. Entertaining, but frequently scary. Mike Deldebbio, a recent Vietnam vet, was a good guy on a good day, who smoked a lot of Statman's weed, which mostly quelled his anxiety and agitation, but occasionally had the opposite effect, resulting in weirdness such as Mike climbing the Barrows field chain link fence, and staying there for innings at a time. Maybe some residual anxiety from his Vietnam days, the need to be on scout patrol, so he could survey the goings on happening nearby on Telegraph Ave. Who knows? I got in a couple of triple headers on back-to-back weekends in November, before the rain came and ended the season. Until mid-February, that is. Life on the west coast. I was loving it.

CHAPTER 5

Lonna, the Not So Prima Donna

All of these distractions - Reno, softball, Ricky, my OSU buddies, and my new Atherton Street housemates - made my grieving regarding Carole's sudden death almost bearable. But like Joe Louis said, when fighting Billy Conn for the heavyweight title in 1941, "He can run but he can't hide." This too was true about my sadness. Regardless of all the socializing, gambling, softball, and mini forays into the world of prostitution, I frequently lapsed into deep sadness, and sometimes depression, particularly when I was alone, which I somehow had contrived to be as little as possible. Even though I wasn't working, I attempted to be as busy as possible. Mostly. Alone in my room, walking back from a cigarette run, or most intensely, when listening to music, the sadness kicked in. Three albums that were of huge significance to my relationship with Carole particularly affected me. All three were super popular while the two of us were falling in love, back in 1971. Cat Stevens' "Tea for the Tillerman," Carole King's "Tapestry," and Marvin Gaye's political breakthrough album, "What's Going On." Any of those three, especially when they came on the radio by happenstance, could send me reeling into puddles of tears. I tried to cry in private, but sometimes, the emotions were too intense and I would break down in front of friends. Luckily for me, my friends were not that macho, and could handle it for the most part. Statman would do his best Marlon Brando as Don Corleone imitation, mock admonishing me to "be a man" as if he were talking to the Johnny Fontaine character in the Godfather, while Ricky, doing his Frank Nitty impression from the Untouchables, saying, "Stop acting like a punk Ness," would function to bring me back to the world. The joking around mostly worked. I did not relate to these guys as insensitive, I knew it was their way of saying, *you gotta go on living in the present and future.* They were right. But I only had so much control over how I felt, which was not that much. Regardless, I did try to keep my grief to myself. And mostly succeeded. Besides, Berkeley offered its own brand of bizarreness and weirdness, which served as another useful distraction whether I liked it or not. Despite the fact that Carole was gone, my libido was still intact. Though I missed her deeply, I would still get "hornier than a two peckered billy goat," as one of my hick dorm mates from OSU used to say. And I was sort of thankful for that. I didn't feel like I was being disrespectful to Carole either, for I knew that she would want me to go on and live my best life, so when I got horny, I felt free to indulge. One day in early December, the opportunity arose again.

Driving down Telegraph Ave in the red Octopus, my Toyota Corona, I was a couple of blocks from my house on a foggy late morning, on my way to make an unscheduled visit to my Rose Lane buddy Hal at his flat in North Oakland, when I noticed a very attractive brunette wearing cut-off jeans, her hair down to her lower back. She was hitchhiking. I couldn't believe my luck, or the fact that nobody had stopped to pick her up. I swerved the Octopus into the right lane, and opened my passenger side window, shouting, "Where you going?"

"North Oakland," she replied, opening my passenger side door.

"Hey, how you doin' today buddy?" she enthusiastically asked. Clearly a southern accent.

"Fine," I said. "What part of the south you from?"

"Texas, near Dallas," she said. "My name's Lonna. You?"

"Arnie," I replied.

"I'm going to College near Shafter in North Oakland," she said, then added, "Hey, you're cute."

I was nervous, excited, and instantly turned on. "So are you," I replied, somewhat breathlessly. "Whaddya do?" I asked stupidly, momentarily not knowing what else to say.

"Well, if you want to know the truth, I'm a hooker. But because I think you're so cute, I'll ball you for free. What do you think of that?"

My heart was pumping out of my chest, and all I could think to say was, "A lot. I think a lot about it."

She said, "Let's go to my place."

Five minutes later we were at her place, getting it on. Lonna was extremely aggressive, and rather expert in her advances and moves. But sweet, too, in her way. It was really fun. And exciting. But especially because of the way it happened. So fast. After the deed was done, Lonna invited me to stay over that night. But not before she said she had to go to work. She was meeting up with a German customer, late in the afternoon, who had solicited her Dominatrix services. I was welcome to watch, she said. There would be a place behind the room where she was performing where I could watch without detection. Not thinking of the ethical breaches, nor the illegality, for which I had little concern, I agreed. We went over to her place of business, not far from where Lonna lived, and when the time came, she hid me in a utility closet, leaving just enough space so I could view the proceedings. The German man was quite meek. Lonna did her thing, wearing her single piece Bavarian corset, with the requisite high black boots and black horse whip. Lonna spoke to the German man in a low, but authoritative tone at first. "Bow down you swine and kiss my boots." And then, ratcheting up her voice and with more force, she said, "You need to be whipped, you low life swine."

"Yes countess, whip me hard. I deserve it," said the German man, eager in his need to be dominated. Lonna then commenced to whipping the man, somewhat gently, but surely, voice rising in sadistic glee. It was an act. The guy seemed to get turned on, but in my naive discomfort, I found the whole thing hysterically funny, and it was all I could do to keep from exploding in laughter and blowing Lonna's cover. I succeeded, but barely.

That was my intro to Lonna. We spent two nights together, and slept together a few times after that. But somehow, maybe because we got along so well, the vibe quickly became more brother-sister. Even though she had a hot body, which I frequently craved, the sexual aspect faded fairly quickly. But she was fun to hang out with. Lonna had a three-year-old daughter, and the two of them often came to the house on Atherton to hang out with me and my roommates. One time, in early December, the house decided to throw a big party, filled with close friends, neighbors, and some strangers. A couple of the strangers, Vinnie and Enoch, had chatted up Rosmary while coming back from school about a week earlier, and had come to the house. Turns out they were a couple of ex-cons living in a communal house off Shattuck, two blocks away. Vinnie, a white guy, and Enoch, a

Black dude, had both been released about a month earlier from San Quentin, each on armed robbery raps. Both had been radicalized while at Quentin. Vinnie, in particular, had been immersing himself in the writings of Wilhelm Reich, and was spouting some of his rhetoric, the political stuff about the evils of capitalism, and the effects it had on the family structure. Stuff that my roommate Steve, a Sociology graduate from Cal, and I, a Sociology graduate to be, were familiar with. We resonated with their words, and invited the two of them and their commune of people to the party. A couple of months later, Vinnie, Enoch, and some of the women living with them, made some headlines. They were members of the SLA, who kidnapped Patty Hearst. Enoch was "Cinque," the leader of the SLA. But for that night, all was well. The party, while raucous, was mostly fun, and came off without incident. But this was simply part of the bizarreness, the weirdness of Berkeley during this period. Lonna, who also attended the party, alerted me to the potential danger of these characters. She didn't like how they were acting towards Rosmary, and Lonna had street smarts. She needed them for survival in her business. She could suss out bad vibes in an instant. Turns out she was right, big time.

CHAPTER 6

Darlene

Lots of distractions were helping me feel pretty good a lot of the time, in momentarily forgetting my grief and sadness. Sex, albeit temporary, was the ultimate distraction, and for me, it worked every time. And possibilities were coming from everywhere. The apartment complex where Ricky lived was owned by a guy from Marin County, and his thirty-year-old son, Dick, who managed the place. Dick was a real one. Pretending to be hip, he was stingy with services and repairs. His saving grace was that his girlfriend, Darlene, who befriended Ricky, and his medical school roommate John, and John's girlfriend Lucy, actually was hip. had just graduated from UC-Santa Cruz, and was about my age. Blonde and willowy, with emerald green eyes, and an open demeanor, she started hanging out at the apartment, particularly when landlord Dick was not around. I could tell she had an uneasy relationship with Dick. She frequently bristled at his attempts to control her. Ricky clearly disdained Dick. But one day, a couple of weeks after Darlene began hanging out with the four of us, Dick showed up. Darlene had shown some friendliness towards me, but she had also done the same with Ricky, so it was nothing special. But when Dick came over the vibes were weird. First off, we somehow got into a conversation about Norman Mailer, who I loved, and Dick hated. Darlene leaned in my direction about Mailer. While a feminist, Darlene had an appreciation for Mailer's unabashed libertine attitudes. She also loved Henry Miller and Anais Nin, two very erotically focused writers. Anyway, Dick and I got into an argument.

"Mailer is a great writer. I don't care if he is an egomaniac, the dude can write. Just check out Armies of the Night for openers," I said to Dick with some venom.

Dick said, "Not even close. All he is a sexist, misogynist pig. A fucking blowhard." Rick and John stayed out of the conversation, merely observing. After Dick left, Ricky and I went for a walk in Golden Gate Park, where Ricky delivered his assessment.

"A case of sexual jealousy, pure and simple," said Ricky. "Dick senses Darlene likes you, and he feels threatened. That's on top of his basic dickness. That conversation was not about Norman Mailer at all, man."

"I think you're right. I think he was misguidedly trying to appeal to Darlene's feminist sensibilities, and doesn't realize that Darlene is drawn to writers with erotic interests, which for her takes precedence over her feminist concerns. The guy misses the boat big time when it comes to understanding his girlfriend," I replied, coming to an easy agreement with Rick on the matter of Darlene and Dick.

The next day, I decided to get on the case. When Darlene came over, I made my move. I invited her to go to a movie with me in Berkeley. She accepted, and then the fun began. Darlene was sweet, bright, fun, and loved sex. And not just doing the deed, but talking about it. She loved reading Anais Nin's erotic sensuous essays, and books, and erotica, and we had numerous conversations about Anais and Henry, who I had begun reading under the influence and persuasion of Ricky, who at this point, was also heavily ensconced with

Henry, consuming "Tropic of Cancer" and "Sexus." It wasn't just the concrete act of sex that enthralled us, it was Henry and Anais Nin's erotic sensibility, their way of seeing the world, where every moment, everything, every person was infused with the possibility of the erotic, the life force, which felt like a passionate and positive way to see life. And as relatively inexperienced twenty-somethings, we went for it big time.

Darlene and I probably spent a month together, maybe twice a week, until strangely, she seemed to get cold feet. I knew she had ambivalent feelings about Dick at best, but in mid- January, all of a sudden, she decided to give Dick a chance again. So that was that. About a month later, I heard that she had broken up with Dick, and decided to go traveling in Europe. After all, she came from a fairly well-off Marin County family, and had saved up enough money from waitressing and living with Dick to take her leave. Which she did. Another lady I never heard from again. Short, but definitely sweet.

During this period, when I was not with Darlene or Ricky in San Francisco, I spent a bunch of time with my OSU friends, Doug and Cal, often getting stoned and listening to music, but frequently just hanging out in my house, especially with my roommate, Steve. He was a stoner, but a fairly responsible guy who had just gotten a warehouse job at Westbrae Grocery, a natural food wholesale place filled with natural grains and all manner of organic foods. While a hippie, Steve was not a vegetarian, nor was anyone else in the house, and seeing as we rotated cooking as part of our collective ethos, everyone pretty much ate everything. This made buying and cooking food relatively simple. The responsibility for doing dishes was shared as well. We didn't emphasize cleaning the common rooms, except for the kitchen. The living room was generally in a state of messiness, and the furniture that Steve, Rosmary and I purchased when we first moved into the place, was fairly ratty. A couple of used lazy boy chairs and leftover love seats filled the fairly large living room space, enough furniture for everyone to sit in the room comfortably at the same time, which typically only happened when we had our one hour weekly house meeting. At these meetings, problems, responsibilities, and the issue of "house dope" was bandied about. I somehow prided myself on the fact that I had never paid for pot my entire life, and as I was a minimal to mild user with limited funds, I didn't want to pay for it. I seemed to be in the majority, as only Rosmary, the heaviest daily user, was interested in sharing the expense. She was outvoted 4-1. That was the extent of the hassles. We all seemed to get along well, and we were responsible with the cooking, and dishes, and mostly had independent lives and activities. Earl, a law student at UC Berkeley, and Rosmary, a senior at UC, were both pretty busy and diligent with their studies. Rosmary was a quiet, somewhat shy girl, and Earl was very busy with his law school study groups, so they weren't around that much. And Kerry was busy with her horses, her boyfriend and her classes, so she was barely home. But Steve was home. And he and I were very simpatico. We smoked a fair amount of dope together, which he provided without complaint. We shared musical tastes as well: folk rock, psychedelic rock, curiosity but minimal knowledge about jazz, and a disdain for hard rock. Most of Steve's friends were either from Glendale, where he grew up, or fellow Sociology majors who he had met at Cal. He had no girlfriend, but was straight. One weekend in early December, Steve and a couple of his male buddies decided they wanted to go to Winterland to see the Grateful Dead. As was the "requirement" for Grateful Dead concerts, we all decided to drop acid. Coming onto the stuff about fifteen minutes into the show, we witnessed and felt Jerry Garcia, also known as Captain Trips, the leader of the Dead, orchestrate and conduct the LSD trips of hundreds of fans in the hall, as if he knew where the mass mind of hundreds of acid heads was at all times. Jerry Garcia seemed to effortlessly use the band and the various shifts in mood and tone to guide the tripped out participants to safety and bliss at all times. He was amazing, and I wasn't the only one who felt that way. Steve and his mates had a similar experience, which we talked about incessantly after we came down. Steve and I processed our trips and the concert for days and weeks after. Steve, with his black, shoulder-length hair, mustache, and easy demeanor, was a good complement for my New York intensity. We got along great, with minimal tension.

While that acid trip at the Dead concert was a blast, in part thanks to Jerry, it turned out to be my last trip. I didn't know it at the time, but apparently I had gotten what I needed to learn from psychedelics, and the psychedelics had served their purpose. And what I learned was basically two things. One, that in the scheme of the universe, we were very small and unimportant, which I interpreted as a positive, for it kept my ego at bay and put things in perspective from then on. Second, it turned me onto the vast beauty of all things, and that the world, its people, its trees, even the man-made things, like cars and buildings were beautiful as well. All a matter of point of view. These insights were powerful to me. Subconsciously, I guess it felt like enough, so the Winterland night became my last psychedelic trip.

At Christmas time, I had a visit from my father, my older brother Dave, and his wife. Dave and Cherise were living in Paris at the time, as Dave was involved with post graduate research there, still searching for jobs as a newly minted Ph.D. in French history. Cherise was a fourth year English grad student researching her dissertation on two writers: George Sand, and George Eliot. While Dad stayed at the Claremont Hotel, the luxury spot on the Berkeley/Oakland border, Dave and Cherise stayed with me at my place on Atherton. Rosmary was back in Cape Cod for the holidays, so her room was freed up, which was fine with Rosmary. Rosmary was pretty loose about that kind of stuff, as were pretty much all of my roommates. It made for pretty easy living. The visit with Dad and my brother and his wife went fairly smoothly, except for the usual pressurizing on the part of Dad about my being out of work. Dad knew I intended to return to college at Cal-Berkeley in the spring, but couldn't resist periodically poking me about being out of work.

"Hey brother, how long are you going to be living the life of Riley?" he would say, his voice brimming with annoyance and impatience.

"Don't know Dad," I would reply, trying to avoid sarcasm and a confrontation. Dad hated indolence. Or, should I say, my indolence. Dad was a bit of a workaholic. He put in sixty-five-hour work weeks, and particularly since my mom's death in 1971, was using his medical practice as his prime distraction from grief, not to mention the rampant womanizing that he began about six weeks after mom died in April of that year. I was sort of sympathetic to him, and in a way, even more so after Carole's death, as I understood, really, for the first time, deep grief, and the loss of someone I loved. Knowing about Carole's recent sudden accidental death, he seemed to restrain himself more than usual. He almost even showed some empathy. Dave, and particularly Cherise, were very empathetic, gently inquiring into how I was doing, how I was feeling, and making themselves available for conversation if or when I felt like talking. For some reason, I didn't want to do it very much. I mostly reserved my most intimate thoughts and feelings for talking with Ricky, who was going through his own brand of darkness. I had also spoken a little bit with Rosmary and Steve. I found people to be mostly respectful, not wanting to intrude, which was a double-edged sword for me, as I did not talk about my feelings about Carole's death easily, and probably needed some gentle prodding, which made it tough. Most people were either reluctant to intrude, or bulls in china shops, which obviously did not make for a safe environment to talk. With the bulls, I would recoil and shut down. But, luckily those kinds of people were few and far between. My dad was that kind of guy, but on this visit, exercised rare restraint and sensitivity, except for periodic anxious inquiries about my employment and career situation.

One day during their visit, we took a ride out to Stinson Beach in Marin County, where I got to experience Dad's height phobia in all its glory. Dad was now in year thirty-six of the phobia, created when he was an intern going out with the ambulances. On one such occasion, he had to climb on the outer stairwell of a thirty-story building in the Bronx to rescue a suicidal man. During this climb, he accidentally made the mistake of looking down on his way up to the top of the building. He got dizzy and nearly fell, and from then on was afraid of heights. The phobia was exhibited on ski slopes, and on our drive on Highway 1, with its treacherous overlooks, on our way to Stinson. Strangely, I found it humorous. Maybe I enjoyed seeing Dad be vulnerable. Height phobia was not my issue. I had other fish to fry, and that was not one of them. And my relationship with Dad was not good enough where I could feel and show true care and concern, as I still mostly felt on my guard around him. So that was that. While they were here, I got the opportunity to be a tourist, which was fun, but after a week with Dad, and ten days with my brother and sister-in-law, I was eager to get back to my life. My life of distraction. My unemployed life, as Dad would put it. But my life as I was living it nonetheless.

Rosmary
(January-March 1974)

January of 1974 gave me a taste of the rainy season in the Bay Area. It rained twenty-two out of thirty-one days. Not that it got cold. Maybe 38 degrees was the coldest. But with the crappy insulation of our house (all the houses in the Bay were a joke in that way), it frequently felt colder, and my roommates and I would walk around the houses with blankets around our shoulders, or stand in front of the heat vent, especially in the mornings when we awoke. We had an unspoken rule about keeping the heat off at night, as none of us liked waking up with that groggy feeling. But the price we paid was freezing until the heat came on in the morning. The lousy weather kept most of us in the house more frequently, and so I got closer with Steve, Rosmary and Earl.

Earl was a character. A southerner from Ft. Worth, Texas, and a Vietnam vet, Earl was raised in the Pentecostal tradition. Vietnam had been his crucible, so while he survived 'in country,' and returned to the U.S. unscathed physically, one major obvious thing that changed was his belief in God. He went from being a fairly big believer to a stone cold atheist, a vehement non-believer. Proof of this happened one day in January, on a rare sunny afternoon that month, as he was walking on Telegraph Ave. After getting a hot dog at his favorite hot dog stand, Top Dog, a fervent, proselytizing Jesus Freak approached him. Looking him straight in the eye with that frenzied true believer look, the Jesus Freak shouted, "Hey. Have you found Jesus?" Without batting an eye or taking a beat, Earl replied, "Have you lost that mother fucker again?"

When Earl relayed that story to me, his face filled up with so much delight and glee that we both cracked up for many minutes. Such was Earl. He was on his way to becoming a criminal attorney. Sharp as a tack, and funny. He genuinely thought I was funny and cool, and while he understood why I was unemployed, he thought that I had too much talent to waste. Somehow, I could hear that from him in a way I couldn't from Dad, or any of the elders for that matter. But that's another story. Now Rosmary. She was another story as well.

Rosmary had chestnut brown hair, and was a shy, quiet, social welfare major at Cal. Sometime in late February, after the rainy season's daily deluge had quieted down some, Rosmary had a visit from a girlfriend who lived on the Cape. Sally was her name. She was blonde and blue-eyed, slightly overweight, and very nice. She and Rosmary had been friends since junior high. Sally crashed in Rosmary's room, and they conspired to take a trip to Arizona and the Mexican border during spring break. Lacking funds, they enlisted my services to help them advertise a window washing service in the Berkeley hills. They posted fliers on the Co-Op grocery store bulletin board, and we were able to secure two jobs, earning about $150 each. Since they would be two girls traveling by themselves, Rosmary asked if I would like to go with them for protection purposes. I agreed, knowing it would be my last opportunity to travel, since in late March

I would be re-enrolling at Cal to finish up my Sociology degree. In mid-March, we climbed into Rosmary's Subaru station wagon and began our trek. Sally, Rosmary and I took turns driving the Subaru. We took it easy, but made it to Needles, California after about nine hours on the road. Hot as hell. Having minimal funds, the three of us stopped at a McDonalds upon arriving, and purchased our burgers, fries and cokes. We didn't have the money for a motel, and all three of us were too tired (and too incompetent) to pitch a tent, so we decided to find a quiet place off the freeway to park the car for the night, and sleep in the Subaru. Needles was hot as hell, even at night. After dinner, Sally lit up a joint, and we shared the stuff. Pretty soon, Sally crashed out. I was in the back seat, all stretched out and fairly stoned, when, to my shock, Rosmary climbed into the back to snuggle up with me. This shy, quiet girl was suddenly very aggressive towards me, and I mean in a sexual way. It's not that I was opposed to this, don't get me wrong. Rosmary was pretty, attractive, and dare I say it, a nice, fun-loving girl. But until this second, I never suspected that she had any interest in me other than as a housemate and friend. The pot was probably the lubricant and disinhibitor, because before I knew it, she and I were going at it pretty hard, getting it on in the back seat. I suspect Sally was woken up by the ruckus, but didn't say anything out of politeness. I also suspect that she was a tad jealous, as the next day, there was a level of tension between her and Rosmary that hadn't existed before. On the other hand, I must say that things between Rosmary and me were quite cozy for the rest of the trip. By day two, we were in Phoenix, where we stopped off to visit a family friend who invited us to dinner. This time, the three of us found a park just outside of town to pitch our tent, and while Sally was still somewhat annoyed at Rosmary, she didn't make a peep when Rosmary and I did our thing that night. The last day of driving got us into Mexico, via Nogales. There, we found a beach on the Gulf of California in a town called Puerto Penasco. The three of us were pretty brazen, not worried about sleeping there until we were awakened in the early hours of morning by a young Mexican guy trying to sell us drugs. Mandrax, in particular. None of us had ever heard of Mandrax. It was only later that we discovered it was another name for Quaaludes. Anyway, Juan was quite persistent. What he wanted in exchange for the Mandrax was Rosmary. After he discovered we weren't married, he kept saying, "I want to buy your See-ster. I give you Mandrax. I give you Mandrax for your see-ster." Well, Rosmary wasn't particularly interested in this arrangement, and the three of us started feeling uneasy, not knowing what other nefarious goings on might be on the horizon, so we hightailed it, as they say in the Westerns, out of there, got in our car, and raced to the border to get back into Arizona. Enough Mexico for the three of us, but plenty of fodder for humorous banter the rest of the trip back. This time, we decided to drive into LA and head up the coast on Highway 1, something neither Sally nor I had ever done before. After plenty of twists and turns and spectacular views, especially in the Big Sur area, we arrived back at Atherton house three days before the start of spring semester. Strangely, Rosmary and I resumed our roommate relationship without having to say a word. Soon after, she hooked up with Gill, a Berkeley musician, and all went on as if nothing had happened. This was fine with me, but sort of unusual. In my experience, it was usually the girl who wanted more of a relationship after sex, but I suppose every generalization had its exceptions. Sex with Rosmary was over, except for one last fling, about a month later. Rosmary got drunk one night when Gill was not around, and made her way into my room. In my infinite horniness, I rarely turned down the advances of a woman and this time was no exception. Drunken sex wasn't that good, but it'll do in a pinch, and I guess I needed a pinch. Rosmary was sweet, but now I knew something of her edges, particularly when intoxicated. When she was with Gill, I felt a twinge of jealousy. I sensed Rosmary felt the same when I was with another girl, and soon her opportunities for jealousy would come more frequently.

Spring in Berkeley was upon us. School was starting and Dewey softball was picking up again. I was ready. And strangely, I had not been thinking about Carole except in quiet moments, which I had somehow conspired to keep as minimal as possible. How could it be that despite having lost the love of my life in a horrible sudden accident, I was actually feeling good, enjoying myself, engaging with friends and now returning to school almost as if nothing had happened? With all my therapy and hospitalizations, I was still more of a mystery to myself than ever. I knew that I had cared for her deeply, but I also knew life went on, and that Carole would want me to get on with my life and be happy. But this soon? It was weird, and Ricky, my Harvard Psych major bud, thought it was weird too. Somehow, he was feeling worse than I was, and no calamitous event had taken place in his life. People were weird. Life was weird.

CHAPTER 8

Statman and the Berkeley Good Vibes

Seeing as how this was Berkeley, California, the weather was so mild that by February, softball season was upon us again. And not a moment too soon. Because all through December and January, during the rainy deluge of those months, I had been reduced to weekly five-on-five indoor basketball games with Ricky and a Harvard mate of his named Greg, who was finishing up his dissertation while working at UC Berkeley. We also played with some other guys in their 30s and 40s. The game was okay, but my asthma made it difficult to run up and down the court for long periods of time, so consequently, our team was the victim of easy fast breaks by the other team. It made the game less interesting. Stupid, if you want to know the truth, but it was a form of exercise. Of course, my smoking (at this point, a pack and a half a day) didn't help my wind or my asthma, more of the stupid if you want to know the truth, but that's the kind of guy I was (am). So when softball season came around, well, that was my kind of sport. Less running! Dewey softball! I had played a couple of times in November, and immediately took to it. All the regulars were back. The Statman, Sol, the great Holdeni, and Victor, the frisbee wizard. World champion frisbee player. All characters, each in their own right, but particularly the Statman, who let it be known that for the third year in a row, he would be keeping official stats on each and every game so that he would be available to let each player know how they were doing. In addition, Statman provided the players with by far the best dope. This year, it was his Hawaiian brand. In previous years, he had shared his famous Colombian and Panama Red, kind of downer paralytic dope if you asked me. But this year's stuff, Hawaiian, also known as Maui Wowie, had a kind of lilt, and a more psychedelic effect. Out of eighteen players, I would say about a dozen partook. Since the game took place at the UC Berkeley women's softball field and P.E. area, there was the extra added benefit of being able to ogle the sunbathers in the right field bleachers on warm spring days. Many of our players, even the righty hitters, would deliberately bat lefty to see if they could uncork their shots into the bleachers, in the hopes that doing so would cause the topless girls to suddenly spring up and leap around in fear. It worked a few times, and was a great source of entertainment. Stoned or not stoned. Because the Women's Movement was peaking, and pervasive in progressive Berkeley circles, it was no longer socially acceptable to cat call at the sight of a beautiful woman. It was devised, I believe, by Dewey, that whenever a beautiful girl went by (and many of them did), we would use the phrase "Major League Scout" to provide cover for our still rampant licentious ways. Sexism had gone underground.

The games, because we were stocked with a lot of excellent players, mostly of good high school level, were very competitive. The pot slowed things down, but still, there was a fair amount of arguing. Most of us were in our twenties, at the height of our athletic prowess, and quite eager and willing to show off. When girlfriends or wives came around, the intensity level would go off the charts. With the presence of a woman, a mellow, stoned out game could suddenly escalate as if it were the 7th game of the World Series. It was funny. But I was a part of these shenanigans as much as any of the other guys, if not more. These guys were just my speed. I liked the diversity of the game too. We had our share of Black guys who played, and from time to time, women played as well. But they didn't stick around all that "yang" energy unless they came partnered up. The games filled up my weekends, and soon my weekdays too, because Dewey, the organizer, got a bunch of us who were out of work and collecting unemployment to form the Berkeley Good Vibes, a UC Berkeley recreation league team, to take on the rest of UC Berkeley softballers. Usually, the other teams represented academic departments, like Chemistry, or Political Science. In a twelve game season spanning eight weeks, the Good Vibes went 11 and 1. We were the favorite to win the playoffs, which featured the top four teams. We won our semi-final game handily, beating Dave Keith and Poli Sci. Dave, usually a quite competent pitcher, easily unraveled when things didn't go his way, which usually happened by the third or fourth inning. Against us, true to form, a bad call by the ump set Dave off, and he proceeded to walk three batters in a row, and then gave up back-to-back homers to Statman and UC Berkeley senior Derek Mills, who was, by the way, on LSD the whole game. Contrary to popular opinion, the acid only helped his performance. Derek hit two homers, including a grand slam to boot. We won 15-3, so now we were in the finals. At the after-game beer fest at La Val's Pizza, he said the softball looked like a soccer ball when he was batting.

In the finals, we faced The Diggery, another motley crew of Cal students, alumni and ringers, including the fastest windmill pitcher in the league, Stan Cozeroff. Similar to Dave Keith in volatility, possessing a crackling sardonic wit, Stan had our number. Despite the fact, or maybe because of the fact, that most of our players were stoned, the Good Vibes, a great hitting team all season, was reduced to popping out or strikeouts. That is, except for me. Stan's fastball went right into my wheelhouse. Knee high and slightly on the inside of the plate, I whacked the ball for two solo home runs, and a third near miss to deep left field. It was not enough though, as The Diggery, who we had destroyed 7-1 in a regular season game, beat us handily in the finals. 5-2. Though I was happy about my two "taters," I was still upset that our heavily favored Good Vibes had gone down to defeat in the league championship. Still and all, softball remained a spring highlight.

Years later, Stan, the Diggery's winning pitcher, and later a restaurant proprietor of none other than the Diggery Inn, who in addition to being sardonic, later became bombastic, would invariably greet me upon entering his restaurant, in full bellow, in front of a packed house of patrons with, "Arnie's here! Arnie hit two home runs off me in a championship league game! Say hello to Arrr-nie." Apparently Stan never forgot it either.

Sociology

Six months after Carole's death, strangely, I was still doing ok. I had my moments, my bad moments, but living in Berkeley, with its myriad of distractions, made life not just bearable, but almost good. So good in fact, that I signed up for three Sociology classes at Cal. OSU approved my last classes, so I would be eligible for graduation by June. Doug Billips, a new OSU friend in the same situation as me, had been out of school about a year and a half, taking his time, hanging out, and doing menial jobs like warehouse clean-up. Doug decided he had had enough of that shit, and it was time to complete the goal. Even though college was more his parents' desire than his, being out of school and out in the world convinced him that life without a degree had its limits. I had arrived at a similar conclusion, but also discovered, with Carole's help, that I could be a good student, and actually enjoy classes if I put my mind to it, which I had back in Columbus. But now, in Berkeley, I wondered if I could summon up the discipline and consistent motivation to finish my degree. I feared I would not be able to concentrate. I hadn't slowed enough to read a book since Carole's death, and I think I associated slowing down with having to confront my sadness and grief about Carole. But now, my good experiences have given me back enough confidence to give it a shot. Besides, Doug and I would meet daily on campus for coffee at the Cafe Med on Telegraph. That helped. I was taking *Sociology of Sport*, taught by the Black activist Harry Edwards, a course unpacking the political, economic, and racial myths and realities surrounding football, baseball and basketball. Given my love of sports, I couldn't go wrong. My next class was Anthony Platt's *Criminology*, a Marxist takedown and analysis of the criminal justice system. Again, my wheelhouse. Finally, Robert Friend's *Social Theory* course, which used Marxist, Freudian and feminist lenses to understand western culture and society. Given those three, I thought I should be home free. All I had to do was concentrate.

Well, I did all right. Enough to get B's. Enough to graduate from OSU with a 3.2. Concentration wasn't as optimal as it had been while I was living with Carole in Columbus, but good enough to get the job done. Of course, there were glitches. Sometimes, when I was trying to study, thoughts about Carole came fast and furious, like an ocean high tide during storm craft warnings. When I experienced memories of our love, I was reduced to a puddle. I tried to let the feelings come. It felt awful, though cleansing somehow. Doug's company at the Cafe Med made it tolerable. He was aware of my situation, and mostly supportive. For the last three years, Doug had been married to a Long Island Jew he met in Columbus, and so far, he had no complaints. He liked to party and smoke dope more than she did, but they had no problems to write home about. He did his share of ogling the ladies, as did I, but again, nothing out of the ordinary.

Meanwhile, on weekends that spring, Ricky, my old friend from second grade, was trying to resurrect his life. He took a job at Tower Records, and with some newly written songs, a backlog of old ones, and some cover versions of Van Morrison, Jesse Winchester, Jackson Browne and John Fogarty, Ricky was ready to take his solo acoustic guitar act back out into the public eye. He found an Oakland spot in Jack London Square called the Rusty Scupper, where he played for nickels and dimes. That didn't matter so much to Rick, as he saw it as part of his reclamation project. Playing for your basic half drunk, half attentive crowd. But Rick was able to gain enough attention to have an impact. Certainly he had mine, as I caught his act practically every weekend, transporting Rick and his equipment in my car from San Francisco. Rick had his own introspective love songs, plus a knack for imitation, doing uncanny impressions of John Fogarty and Van Morrison's vocalizations, almost to a tee. I enjoyed watching Rick thoroughly, glad to see he was making a comeback from his Hawaii debacle, and getting back into his music. Additionally, occasionally there were attractive women in attendance. One Saturday night in late April, I made a new acquaintance. Or should I say, she made mine. A moderately attractive brunette with a nice body eyed me, and smiled when I eyed her back. Continuing to smile, I was mandated to walk from my table to hers to strike up a conversation. Tammy was her name, and she was with a bunch of other people. As I grabbed a chair, she made it more than clear that it was okay to sit down and chat her up. Initially, we chatted about Ricky's set. She liked him a lot. She was very forward, and informed me that she was a hooker, and would love to get me into bed, for free, just like my past experience with Lonna. I gave her my number, after informing her that I would have to take Rick back to San Francisco that night around midnight. Returning to Berkeley around 1:30am, buzzed but not drunk from a couple of beers, I was lying down, trying to get some sleep, when the phone rang. Steve answered, and informed me that there was a Tammy on the line. When I picked up the phone, in an insistent, semi-intoxicated tone, she said, "I want to come over tonight and fuck your brains out."

Well, what could I say? I couldn't think of a good reason to say no, and the horndog that I was, could only come up with, "Yes."

Fifteen minutes later, Tammy, who lived in North Oakland, was knocking on my door. I was half awake, and Steve, with sort of a pissy attitude, showed her into my room. Without so much as a hi, hello, or how are you, she began doing her thing. Like the pro that she was, she got the job done with dispatch. I did my best to service her with mixed success. Then, we both collapsed into an intoxicated sleep. The next day when I awoke, she was gone. A role reversal if ever I saw one. But, to be honest, I was not unhappy to see her go. I loved a shtup with minimal verbiage. Not that we would have had that much to say to each other anyway. Another good distraction for the Arnie man.

CHAPTER 10

Change is Afoot

It was great having Ricky around. We had spent more time together in the last eight months than we had since we were kids in grade school. Now we had gotten to know each other's nuances and subtleties more intimately than ever before. Ricky got to see my mercurial, impulsive, brusque, and frequently moody manner, and I got to see how obsessive, ruminative and anxious Rick could be, although with his recovery from the debacle in Hawaii, the outward manifestation of Rick's anxiety and obsessiveness began to subside. It helped that Rick saw a therapist who focused on the body and the breath, which may have forced him to slow down and be more in his body. After a few months, including his time playing at the Rusty Scupper, Rick's confidence came back. When he received a call from a friend who co-ran Interlaken, an international music and arts camp in New Hampshire, and was invited to be a counselor there, Rick jumped at the chance. I think he saw it as a way to make a clean start, and maybe get back to the East Coast. Rick, at this time, saw his life as a kind of climbing up a hill, and opening up a hot dog stand at the top of the hill (metaphorically speaking, of course). Until now, he had continually fallen from the hot dog stand because the foundation he was standing on was made of sand. With his newfound wellbeing, Rick now began to feel that he could climb up to the top of the mountain again and rebuild his hot dog stand, only this time on more solid ground. I was glad for his newly regained confidence, but sad to see him go. He was my oldest friend, and friends like that didn't grow on trees, to put it mildly.

Luckily, in the middle of June, a day before Rick left for New Hampshire, reinforcements came in the form of my younger brother Lew, coming out from Madison, Wisconsin to spend the summer with me and attend classes at UC Berkeley. Just in time, too. Change was afoot at the Atherton Street house, as the lease was up, and housemates were dispersing. Earl went off to room with other law school mates, Rosmary went back to Cape Cod upon graduation, and lastly, Steve, went off to Santa Barbara on a work transfer. These moves left me having to hustle up another place to live, which I succeeded in doing fairly quickly. This time, I was with seven other roommates in a more suburban setting in Kensington, the town next to Berkeley. The house I secured was far less charming, a more modern 1950's ranch-style house. Luckily, my friend Hal, my Rose Lane buddy from OSU, and his girlfriend, also needed a place to live, so with Lew, I only needed 4 more people to fill the six bedroom house. I found another couple, Mormon newly-weds, extremely nice and responsible, and another single guy and female, and we were set. Moving date was July 1. It was cumbersome getting everybody moved in, and immediately after the eight were settled in, we had a house meeting to decide on both shared responsibilities, and whether to buy house dope, a previous sore point at Atherton. Like at Atherton, the distribution of cooking and cleaning duties went smoothly, but I was a minority of one voting no on house dope. I was a casual user at best, while everyone else at the house was a daily smoker. Even the Mormon couple resented this, but went along with having to support other people's habits. Somewhat worried about money, I had now been out of work going on nine months, and I was getting tired of it. Though glad that I had used some of that time to finish college, increasingly I was feeling back to myself mentally, and as such, getting somewhat restless, even bored at times. Only occasionally did I tear up when thinking of Carole, but even though I hadn't found anyone who came close to embodying all of Carole's wonderful qualities, and deep capacity to get me, my sexual dalliances had succeeded in distracting me in the way I thought I needed. But now, with school done, I began thinking about what was next. I decided against returning to Rose Lane. It didn't pay enough, and wasn't permanent, but I was definitely thinking about the mental health field. Even though I was getting tired of being out of work, there were new distractions which played to my indolence. Primarily, I was focused on the impeachment hearings. And like me, my brother Lew, and everyone in my family were all political junkies. We all kept rather close tabs on the goings on in Washington regarding our sworn enemy, Richard Nixon, whom Lew and I hated with a vengeance. There was a lot to stay focused on. The summer was tailor made for our rapt attention on the hearings, blow by blow. I now had something to do, and Lew was equally addicted and made for interesting and hilarious company.

Of course, we did get out of the house, with weekend jaunts to Santa Cruz and Big Sur, and attendance at Dewey softball, where some of the stoned-out regulars, who couldn't remember Lew's name, referred to him as 'Young Arnie.' Lew impressed my softball friends, as his solid wrist hitting, good reflexes and capable infield abilities made him more than above average by the game's standards. Lew, a sports fanatic, teamed up with Doug Billips, who still needed one class to graduate, and they took Harry Edwards' *Sociology of Sport* together. A favorite of lefties of all stripes and colors, the class was both provocative, and a relatively easy A.

Despite Lew's presence, along with Hal and girlfriend Rebecca, the collective arrangement was not as much fun this time. Atherton had been new and exciting, and a great intro into Berkeley life, despite my grief over Carole. My roommates had been warm, and we all shared a sense of connection. The new place on Hanson Lane in Kensington was chaotic, with not enough privacy, too much noise, and not enough easy connection with the other housemates. Something was off. I wasn't really happy there, but I was also too lazy to do anything about it. Besides, I had just moved, so I put up with it, and focused my attention on the impeachment hearings. It was not hard. The hearings were riveting.

CHAPTER 11

The Hearings

For about a month, from mid-July to mid-August, when Lew would get back from his classes, I turned on the TV set every time Peter Rodino, the Democratic chairman of the House Judiciary committee, called the hearings to order. As it was a Democratically controlled House of Representatives, there were several more Democratic members on the committee than Republicans. Some of the house members were memorable. For the Dems, Barbara Jordan, Elizabeth Holtzman, and Charles Rangel stood out. Barbara Jordan, for her eloquence and air of moral authority when she thundered against Nixon's brazen hypocrisy and disrespect for the law. Elizabeth Holtzman, because she was Jewish, from Brooklyn, and spoke with lawyerly precision, was another favorite. Lastly, Charles Rangel, a new Black Congressman from the Harlem district (Adam Clayton Powell's old seat) was popular with Lew and me for his outrage, and most importantly, because for some strange reason, we both found it amusing to hear a Black man talk with a New York accent. Go figure. Lew and I were weird, and shared a bent sense of humor. But as entertaining and affirming as the Dems were to the both of us, they paled in entertainment value to the insane rantings of some of the Republicans. We looked forward to Charles Sandman,

Republican from New Jersey, every time he spoke. We predicted with high accuracy how he would preface his remarks. "Isn't it amazing," Sandman would begin, as he would attempt, unconvincingly at least to Lew and I, to attack the democrats' hypocrisy and blatant "witch hunting" of that great man Richard Nixon. Fabulous to watch Sandman's effort, but actually laughable, pathetic even. And when the seventeen minute tape, directly implicating Nixon, was released, we had our "smoking gun." From there it was just a matter of time. Nixon tried to get his Republicans to stick with him, but when Barry Goldwater, the so-called "conscience of the conservative movement" said he would vote to convict to Nixon's face, the handwriting was on the wall for the tricky man. The next day, Tricky came on TV to announce his resignation, his way of avoiding impeachment and conviction. In Berkeley, on the evening of August 8,1974, just minutes after Nixon resigned, Telegraph Avenue, the heartbeat of Berkeley activism, erupted. Hundreds descended on the street in a spontaneous display of joy and elation. The Fifth Estate's version of "Ding Dong the Witch Is Dead" could be heard blaring from apartments. Gender be damned. Nixon was gone. Lew and I got there ourselves, wondering in curiosity whether there would be a celebration and we were right. Good instincts. Clearly one of the most fun nights of the summer. But not the only fun night.

At the Oakland Coliseum, we caught Vida Blue going against Gaylord Perry, A's vs. Cleveland Indians. Perry, with a 16-1 record, was deemed unbeatable. The game went 11 innings before 55,000 fans, ending in a pinch-hit single by Berkeley's own Claudelle Washington in his first major league game, icing on the cake of a well-played, tense, close game. But the piéce de résistance of Lew's stay with me that summer was an invitation by Bill Cody, a friend of Doug Billips, to DJ a set on his KTIM nightly show in San Rafael. Cody, another

Buckeye buddy of Doug's, was a fledgling rock DJ trying to secure a regular gig on a mainstream station. He had landed a fill-in spot in San Rafael with a local station with a small but dedicated rock music following. Cody had befriended me via Doug that spring, and we had already gone to a few rock concerts together. There was Van Morrison and Jerry Garcia at the Keystone in Berkeley, a smallish music venue, which we hit in part because Cody idolized Van Morrison. Everybody loved Jerry Garcia in the Bay Area, which went without saying. And in early June, we went to Day on the Green, a Bill Graham extravaganza at the Oakland Coliseum featuring The Dead, The Beach Boys, and Commander Cody, where for the first and only time in my life, I got to walk on a major league field, feel the green grass, and look up at the stands from field level. Filled me with goose bumps. Numinous. The concert was good, too. But I was pretty stoned, so that made it a little less fun. The dope was too strong.

That was my intro to Cody, a total rock music fanatic, with a silvery smooth voice perfect for FM radio. A sweet guy to boot. One night, a week before Lew was to leave to return to Madison for his junior year, Cody invited Lew and I to his station in San Rafael to program a set. After some deliberation, we launched with, "Wouldn't it Be Nice" by The Beach Boys, "Love and Happiness" by Al Green, and "Natural Woman" by Aretha Franklin. Lastly, we added Lou Reed's "Sweet Jane." The live version. We were proud of ourselves for our musical taste. People called in to applaud our set choices as well. Jane, the KTIM newscaster and friend of Cody's, said, "You guys hit a home run with every one of your choices, and especially your ending with Lou Reed. Very dramatic." Her call felt particularly good, as Jane's musical taste was held in high esteem by Cody. If Jane liked our set, then it must have been good. But as good as that night was, it held a kind of bittersweet taste, for I knew that in a few days Lew would be leaving town. In a sense, leaving me to my own devices. Since Carole's death, I had had my mainstay people with me. First, Ricky for an unplanned visit, then Lew, for a planned stay. Their presence made coping with my grieving a lot easier. But then, there was a graduation party for Doug Billips and I the night before Lew left town, and it was there that I lucked out once again.

CHAPTER 12

Delphine

There must have been at least thirty people at Bill and Muff's party that night in San Rafael. Half the people there I knew, some I kind of recognized, and some I didn't know at all. In that in-between category of kind of recognized was this young, sparkly, blue-eyed, sprightly woman with dirty blonde hair and a blue work shirt, sitting in lotus position on the floor, as were several other people attending the party. Bill and Muff didn't have a lot of furniture, and it was the custom of us counterculture, hippie types to enjoy gatherings sitting on the floor with legs crossed, bopping to the music, beer in hand, usually stoned. Tonight was no different. The vibe was raucous yet mellow, both Doug and I celebrating our belated degrees. Doug's took seven years, and mine, six. Not that unusual, then. We were not in a hurry to find careers. We were interested in having a good time, exploring. And that's what we were doing. But with Lew leaving the next day, for me, the celebration offered mixed feelings. I knew I would be all right, or so I told myself, but I had not really been alone since Carole's death, and now I would be. I told myself this would be a challenge. But hey, not so fast, for this sparkly, blue-eyed woman was making heavy stoned eye contact with me, and it was quite a rush. After a bit, I realized who Delphine was. She had been the girlfriend of Greg, one of my Berkeley Good Vibe teammates.

When I started chatting her up, she quickly mentioned that Greg was in LA for the summer, having just graduated Cal, leaving the field somewhat ambiguous as to Delphine's status. Women were like that. Indirect. Flirtatious, but often not clear. Leaving it up to me to probe. The contact with Delphine that night was intense. We conversed easily, with some undeniable sexual tension. The next day, after bidding Lew adieu at the Oakland airport, I got Delphine's address from Bill who knew her well from Columbus. I did my usual no call, just show up number. Delphine lived in South Berkeley with three other people; the landlord, and two others. The landlord was a sweet guy named John, a super mellow Harvard grad, who answered the door when I knocked and asked for Delphine. As luck would have it, Delphine was home, in her room listening to jazz. She gave me a warm greeting and a hug. She offered me a beer and a J. The conversation with Delphine flowed easily. We had Ohio State in common, and we had both left Columbus without a degree. She had arrived in Berkeley about a year earlier than I. She loved it here. She was trying to get into doing stained glass, as she had been a fine arts major at OSU. She too had left Columbus with only a quarter left, but her circumstances had been different. She had been fleeing a marriage to a local Columbus FM DJ, Kenny Groat, an underground music celebrity with excellent taste. Even though she got out of Columbus in a hurry, things with Kenny were still friendly. Delphine realized she was too young, only twenty-one at the time of the marriage, and she wanted to be single. Kenny was heartbroken, which Delphi, as she preferred to be called, mentioned with a slight hint of haughtiness. She knew her effect on men. Knowing that Bill and Muff were in the Bay Area, along with Doug and Irene, made Berkeley the perfect place for her to land, especially with Berkeley's counterculture repu-tation. Delphi was in the process of seeking work at a stained-glass warehouse in South Berkeley, and signed up to finish up her last quarter at Cal as well. An OSU tradition, it seemed. Anyway, Delphi was sooo cute and sexy. Made great eye contact. And she smoked unfiltered Camels to boot. A little tough girl in a pixie frame. Just adorable. I must say, I was bowled over by Delphi's charm and viva-ciousness, of which she had a ton. She liked me too. During my visit, she seemed to indicate that she and Greg were not really a couple, or at least not exclusive, opening the door for yours truly. A few tokes into the visit, the guardrails came down, and we were clenched in an embrace, and pretty soon, not just that. The sex was memorable. Hot and intense. From that day on, we were inseparable. Being with Delphine made me want to get off unemployment, which I had been on for ten months now. Not that that was unheard of. The country had been going through an oil embargo, and the unemployment rate had spiked pretty high. People were allowed to be on unemployment insurance for as long as sixty-five weeks. I had only used forty by this time, so I was in good shape as far as that went, but getting antsy. Delphine's artistic ambition and focus motivated me. Later that week, back at the pad, my buddy Hal informed me of a new psych ward opening up in Martinez, at the Contra Costa County hospital. "What is different about it," Hal said, "is that the place is going to be run by this radical therapist by the name of Stan Meyerson, who specializes in doing family therapy with the families of psych patients on the unit." Even more importantly, at least from my perspective, given my background, Hal said, showing some excitement, "Taking medication will be completely voluntary, actually de-emphasized." And the best part was that Mayerson was looking for people who had been hospitalized, or had psychotic breaks, to be part of the staff, and even to be taught how to do family therapy. This totally excited me, as I was looking for a career, and of course had been both psychotic and hospitalized four times already. The Mayerson situation represented the possibility of something interesting to do to at least pay the bills while I figured out what I really wanted to be when I grew up. I contacted Mayerson, and he set up an interview with me for the following day. The unit would be opening in May of 1975, in about nine months, so it wouldn't be right away, he said. Meeting with Mayerson was great. He took a liking to me, and was intrigued by my background. Not put off or frightened, he thought I could be a real asset to the place. There was only one kicker. This would be a county job, so under the auspices of the Civil Service. I would have to meet their requirements, but Mayerson, a slick talking, ex-New Yorker, thought he could get around any obstacles they might present. He told me to get back to him in March, and by then, he would know for sure. I was thrilled, thinking this could be a real opportunity. Delphi was excited for me too, even though she was not bothered in the slightest by my being out of work. After all, I was trying to figure things out. The only difference between Delphi and me, she figured, out loud, that is, is that she knew what she wanted to do, and was ready to go for it. Discussions of work and career were only part of what was happening between us, particularly in those early months of our relationship in August and September. We went to a lot of shows, and did some really cool camping in exotic locations. Delphi was heavily into jazz, and in quick succession, took me to see Sonny Rollins, Mose Allison, and Keith Jarrett, all three of which I loved.. Then, the week after Labor Day, we took a hiking trip up to Desolation Wilderness, a relatively untraveled stretch of country south of Lake Tahoe in the Sierras, where for the first time, I backpacked. Delphi and I shlepped our packs, carrying three days of food, a Swiss army knife, and sleeping bags about three miles into the wilderness until we hit Smith Lake, a pristine, turquoise beauty. What was amazing, wonderful, and slightly scary was that there wasn't a soul in sight. Just us. I packed my Krishnamurti book, recommended by my old Reno casino mate, Bill Johnson, and Delphi brought "Diet for a Small Planet," the new bible for a vegetarian lifestyle. No radio or TV, just those two books, nature, and ourselves for three days. It was beyond ecstatic. A new relationship and new experiences. What could be better? Bliss city.

CHAPTER 13

Kensington Part 2

From the beginning, Delphine and I were inseparable. We spent not one night a week together, but six. By three weeks into the relationship, we both decided that we wanted to move in together, but not in the places where we already were living. More luck would come our way. Statman, my new softball buddy, mentioned one day in mid-September, that the house he was living in in Kensington, a three bedroom, had a space coming open. I told him I was interested, and would be bringing my new girlfriend. Not a problem for the Stat. Actually, the more Stat and I talked or hung out after softball, the more we realized we had in common. We were on the same wavelength, not just in terms of knowledge and interests but likes and dislikes, almost as if I had found my twin. We anticipated each other's mental associations especially in the realm of sports and movies. Lots of good-natured egging each other on, particularly about our favorite baseball teams. Stat was a died-in-the-wool Yankee fan, and I was a heartbroken Brooklyn Dodger fan before the Dodgers cruelly left Brooklyn for the west coast. Whenever I would extol Dodger greats of yesteryear, like Duke Snider or Jackie Robinson, Stat, with all of the ludicrous brutality he could muster, would recite, "1941, 47, 49, 52, 53, 56," the years the Yanks beat the Dodgers in the World Series. Mocking me. Taunting me. It was funny and ridiculous. The connection, the competition. Like brothers, but closer in a weird way. Stat started referring to me as his twin, or Doppelgänger from the Bizzarro world, a reference to a world from Superman comics where everything was backwards or inverted. It was funny. Maybe it was true. I presented the news about moving in with the Stat to Delphine and she went for it big time. Our move-in date was October 1. Meantime, I let my housemates on Hanson Way know I was outta there. I had some guilt about leaving the situation there so soon, particularly towards my friend Hal, who I had recruited for the house, and had looked forward to living with, but the scene up there was too chaotic, and besides which, although I was congenial with Hal, I did not feel the same towards his girlfriend, Rebecca, who I found abrasive. The woman was hard to tolerate. Couched in her aggressive Feminist ball-busting rhetoric, she frequently accused Hal or me of sexist behavior, rightly or wrongly. Monitoring our speech for signs of chauvinism, and often finding evidence, her form of criticism was way too harsh, and one more reason I was glad to be out of there. Delphine's situation was a little different. She had a nice relationship with landlord John, and while sad to be leaving that situation, she knew that John would have no trouble renting her room. So, consciences relatively clear, we were all set. But just to throw a mini monkey wrench into the proceedings, a week before we were to move into Stat's place, I got a letter from the unemployment office informing me that there was a job they were requiring me to take if I wanted to retain my unemployment insurance. The job was working as a spray painter inside the West Oakland post office, a district office. Huge in size. The pay would be $2.40 an hour. Minimum wage. Unemployment would be withheld while doing this temporary job. So for the next six weeks, including the first month Delphine and I would be in Stats house, I would be schlepping in my Red Octopus to West Oakland to assist in painting the mail room cases where the mail was slotted before the mail deliverers went on their daily routes.

The job turned out to be surprisingly, deliriously fun. First off, at the post office, the workers were predominantly Black. Second off, my crew, which consisted of seven other guys, was all Black. Third off, every day before work, during breaks, lunchtime, whatever, the crew, including me, would get lit. Stoned. And the shit I was smoking, provided by the captain of the crew, was strong as hell, way over my head in terms of what I was used to, making it hard to focus, but conversely making the ongoing verbal patter amongst the crew completely hilarious. Although I was the token white dude, I was seemingly accepted, and found myself assimilating somewhat into the Black culture. Not a problem for me. Black culture was actually preferable. Of course, I didn't have to live what it was like to be Black in America on an everyday basis. I was enjoying the good side without the hard side. By the end of the six week project, I was speaking the Black idiom almost automatically and eating hot links regularly for lunch at the local west Oakland bodega. Not too bad for a minimum wage job. I would say I made the best of it and had great fun. Being stoned on the job afforded me the opportunity to think about what I wanted to do with my life, while only having to be minimally focused on the job itself. Making sure the white spray paint landed on the cases and not the floor, and remembering to put tarp under the cases was pretty easy work. I could space out once I learned the basics of the job, and fantasize about what I wanted to do with my life.

I had dabbled on and off with acting, and the art form retained a fascination. I first took drama class in 9th grade with Mr. Feist, who had, that year, founded the Roundabout Theatre in New York City. I attended class at his new school for one session, until I was overwhelmed by homosexual panic, by the flagrant gayness of the other actors, teachers, and what seemed to be gay exercises. I fled and never returned. Then in college, at OSU, I got involved in Guerilla theater during campus protests: the famous monk robe, pig on casket march, and pig drop off at the CIA booth during a recruitment event in 1970. There was also my ongoing fanatical love of film, particularly the actors Bogart, Brando, Clift, and Newman. My big four. I never forgot that Mr. Feist, in 9th grade, was impressed with my improvisational abilities, and told me I had the potential to be the next Brando. In retrospect, maybe it was a marketing tool to get me to go to his school, but I wanted to believe it. So now, ten years later, I was finally gonna take him up on it, and see what my mettle was. I heard about a school in Berkeley offering Method Acting instruction by a disciple of Stella Adler, Brando's teacher. I decided it was now or never. I enrolled in Jean Shelton Acting School's fall classes during the last two weeks I was painting the post office cases, in early October. Luckily, the classes were at night. Shelton's intro scene study would help me to see if I was good enough, and if acting was what I really wanted to do. Having a focus felt good. That, in addition to the potential job working at the psych ward in Martinez, made me feel like I was finally getting some direction. Being with Delphine was a catalyst. Knowing I had some direction made pot smoking more fun and less anxiety ridden than it had ever been.

The pot smoking and fun I had at the post office created a new feeling of security about smoking dope. It initiated a rather intense pot smoking period for me. Delphine liked to get stoned at least three times a week after work, and the Statman, who always had great and varied strands of dope, was stoned multiple times every day. He stayed lit. And it mostly didn't seem to bother him. He experienced an occasional paranoid, angry rant, but who didn't have those?

CHAPTER 14

Late for the Sky (November 1974)

With the job ending in late October, and my unemployment reinstated, I continued to wait on the status of my hospital psych job, and I was now free to pursue acting classes and not have to worry about seeking a job for the time being. I decided to take piano lessons as well, for the first time since the age of fifteen. But not to play classical music, as I had been directed to play as a kid; this time I would learn blues piano, if I could. My preference. As Stat, a somewhat adroit piano player himself, possessed an old Steinway piano in the basement of the house, it made for a perfect set up to practice. Delphine had secured full time employment at Nervo Stained Glass, a wholesale glass factory in the flatlands of Berkeley, the industrial area, and set up shop for her own stained glass work in Stats unused garage. My schedule was working out nicely as well. I went to acting classes one night a week, and then scene practice for a couple of days during the week to work on the assigned, two-person scene with another student. Then, there were weekly piano lessons with a teacher who emphasized learning blues piano, and of course, the requisite daily practice. Dewey softball was on the weekends, two seven-inning doubleheaders every Saturday and Sunday. Statman and I participated, and frequently drove together. A nice life. Kind of like summer camp for adults with time set aside to really figure out if acting was gonna be the thing for me. Of course, all of this stuff I was doing was accentuated by regular afternoons of getting stoned, sometimes to paralyzing effect, other times to stimulating effect. All depending on my mood, the circumstances of the day, and all the other usual variables that dictated whether the stoned experience would be positive or not. On weekends, Delphine and I and Statman and his girlfriend Erin would attend jazz concerts. Chick Correa, Return to Forever, and Cecil Taylor were some of the more memorable performers we saw.

Jean Shelton was a fabulous acting teacher. At times intensely critical, at times intensely empathetic and gentle, she seemed to have an instinctive sense about who her students were as people, what they could handle and what they needed to further their acting chops. One time when I was doing a scene from Pinter's "The Caretaker," I was required to be lying face down on the floor. Sensing that I was too inhibited, and not letting out my anger, which the scene called for, she pounced on my back and wouldn't let me up until I was genuinely pissed, the primal emotion she was after. Her class was a little like being in psychoanalysis in the service of the acting craft, an aspect of what was involved with the Method. I found it enthralling, and sensed I had some raw talent. Maybe not the next Brando, as my ninth-grade drama teacher had said, but some talent nonetheless. It was clear that I needed a lot of work and dedication to hone the craft if I was going to be successful. I was up for it. With the piano lessons, it was not quite the same. While taken with the blues, when it came to practicing, for some reason my old bad habits kicked in. Procrastinating and minimal work on the lessons became the mode.

Not a good recipe for progress. I told myself that acting was where I wanted to put my energy. The piano lessons lasted four months, and then finito. The acting classes continued.

On the home front, conflict emerged between Stat and a new roommate, Ben, over the blaring of music. Ben, an apprentice electrician, had to be up by 5:45 every morning, so had to be asleep by 10pm at the latest. That's when Stat was just getting started, as he had plenty of money, being independently wealthy, so tension flared up between Stat and Ben over the noise level. It created an environment that could be pretty unbearable at times, and resulted in Delphine and I fleeing to our room for frequent respite from the tension. When Delphine was not working on her stained glass, she and I would be in our room playing our stereo, albeit low enough to be considerate toward Ben. However, this made our interactions a little more claustrophobic than we would have liked, and started to bring out our differences in disposition and style a little more quickly than might have been natural. Delphine was a cheerful, up, extremely positive person, who had little tolerance or desire for the dark side or the negative. I, on the other hand, was quite frequently moody, angry, negative, and cynical. Our differences felt like an unexpressed obstacle or impasse between us. It was hard to talk about. Delphine didn't like a lot of conflict or tension. I was not averse to talking about problems. This difference in and of itself was a problem. It led to a lot of lapses into superficiality. She probably saw me as a negative Ned. At least, that's what she would call me.

One night towards the end of November, after Thanksgiving, the problem crystallized. We were stoned and listening to the new Jackson Browne album, "Late for the Sky." The title song described perfectly how I was feeling. I was idealizing her, but maybe not seeing who she really was, and vice versa. The lyrics and tone of the song left me with an empty, sad, and deeply alienated feeling. Undeniable. It marked the end of our so-called honeymoon with each other. That intense, other person can do no wrong, everything about them is cool, fascinating, and lovable hot phase was over. Reality was now beginning to come into view. Jackson Browne's album hit like an emotional knockout punch. The soul mate I thought I had found was something else. Another human being with her own unique characteristics. Some in sync with mine and some vastly different. Time would tell whether we would make it work. The Jackson song felt prescient. I hoped it wasn't so, but my gut said it was. Meanwhile life went on, and we would find out what's what.

While time was going by, and I was discovering the what's what of it all in my life with the Jean Shelton stuff, the Delphine stuff, and the Dewey softball stuff, I managed to pick up a couple of recipes from the Statman, a fine amateur cook in his own right, who understood what tasted good. I learned about linguine and clam sauce, spaghetti and meat sauce, salmon, baked chicken, pan-fried chicken, and chicken puttanesca, dishes that would serve me in my burgeoning cooking arsenal, and please the rest of the house when we ate together, which was frequent. Because of the ongoing tension, when Ben was around, he rarely ate with us, but Erin and David and Delphine and I frequently did, and David and I often rotated the cooking duties, followed by ample tokes of pot or lines of cocaine, which was becoming part of the after-dinner mix. Stat and Delphine, because of their mutual love for and interest in jazz, had more in common musically. I was basically a rock and roll guy with occasional Broadway musicals and classical thrown in for good measure. Folk, folk rock, psychedelic rock, soul, and r&b were my mainstays, and I was accused, mostly good naturedly, but also accurately, of having pedestrian or philistine tastes. Stat and I and Delphine and

Stat seemed to have more to talk about than Delphine and I. Mostly, between Delphine and I, the sex was the glue. And that was still fabulous. For now, enough.

CHAPTER 15

Tit for Tat
(Christmas 1974)

With the coming of the Christmas holidays, I had my first flush of homesickness. Homesickness for New York. I hadn't been home since Carole and I had visited back in June of 1971 at the beginning of our love affair, so I finally felt ready to visit my homeland. Dad would be in New Rochelle, and Dave and Cherise, in from Paris, where Dave was doing a postdoc while Cherise was finishing up her doctorate. Lew, in the middle of his junior year at Madison, would also be home. So the family would all be together, really for the first time since Mom's death three and a half years earlier. I was excited, and a little disappointed that Delphine wouldn't be accompanying me. She had just started her new job, so that made traveling with me impossible, but I was excited to see family and old friends. Ricky would be there, now living in New York City and in a relationship with Sarah, a dancer he met while counseling at an art camp the previous summer, and doing social work in the Bronx at a city hospital. Mark, another old buddy, was on his way to Berkeley. His three-year marriage was in tatters. Glad to be free, but unsure what was next, he would be awaiting me upon my return from my holiday.

Finally, there would be Mack, another buddy from high school days; baseball, the race track, girlfriends, and forays into marijuana and the underground music scene in Greenwich Village, who I hadn't seen since college visits to Boston, more than three years earlier. A kind of old home week.

I didn't hesitate to see them, minimizing my time with my difficult Dad as much as possible, particularly given that I was out of work with no concrete career direction. His interrogational style had not changed. I spent more time with my older brother, and sister-in-law, and younger brother Lew, who were much easier to be with, and with whom I had much more to say. But the most of my time was spent in Manhattan seeing Ricky.

Ricky was living in Manhattan with Sarah, on Central Park West in the low 80s, and trying to decide what he was going to do. He was torn between a career in psychology, his major at Harvard, and his true love, rock music. Rick had a shitload of songs written by this time, and while not at his social work job in the Bronx, tried to secure gigs, playing for free in various New York bars and nightclubs. He was quite jovial, mostly in a good place, happy to be in a relationship with a woman who seemed quite nice, friendly, and into Ricky, at least to my naked eye.

My friend Mack, on the other hand, seemed in a more intense place. Having secured a position at Capital Records as an A & R talent hunter, and married for two years and living downtown, he was doing a lot of drugs. A lot of pot and a lot of cocaine. For reasons unknown to me, our contact wasn't as warm and tight as it had been in previous years. I wasn't sure what it was about, but chalked it up to drug use. I couldn't think of any other explanation. It's not like we'd had a falling out or anything. But one never knew about these things, particularly when it came to guys, who I realized weren't the most communicative when it came to uncomfortable feelings.

With Ricky, however, who had just spent eight months in Berkeley, it was as if no time had passed, and we took up where we left off. The contact was satisfying and stimulating, like always.

A couple of days after Christmas, during a phone call with Delphine, she casually mentioned that her ex-husband, Kenny Groat, was out visiting from Columbus, and staying with my friend Doug Billips. He had invited her to go to LA for a couple of days, to return the day before New Year's Eve. While in my gut I had a kind of uncomfortable feeling, I did not want to seem uncool, so I told her it was ok. This was mostly not true, but I was trying to convince myself and Delphine. I would pay for not listening to my intuition.

After returning to the Bay on the 30th of December, late that night while Delphine and I were in our room, she made a confession.

"Arnie, there's something I need to tell you," she said.

I felt a sense of dread, something bad in her tone, but all I said was, "What?"

"When Kenny and I were in LA, we slept together one night. It was a mistake. It never should have happened. I realized that I'm not in love with him anymore. But it happened, I'm sorry."

I was stunned. I didn't say anything for a while, and then, stifling some anger, I said, "Are we all right? I don't get it."

"It was a mistake," said Delphine. "I fucked up. It's you I love. I hope you can forgive me."

"I'll try," I said, but I was seething underneath. "It will take awhile," I added. "I'll try. But this hurts."

"Yeah, I don't know what I was thinking. You know Kenny and I are friends, but I realized that he's still in love with me, and wanted to get back together, and I guess I just gave in to the moment. But I realized that I'm not in love with him anymore. I'm in love with you." Meanwhile, while Delphine was talking, I plotted my revenge. Being an Old Testament kind of guy, I reasoned to myself that's what's good for the goose is good for the gander. If she can fuck around, so can I. One day in early January, with Delphine away in Sonoma for a day-long stained glass workshop, I seized the opportunity, and went looking for action.

That afternoon, a cold, windy, rainy Tuesday, I hit the Cafe Med on Telegraph Ave, the place where the activists of the Berkeley Free Speech Movement met to plot out strategy back in 1964. It had a mellow, if not fairly dank, dark vibe, and on this day, I went in alone, ordering black coffee, my usual, and sat at a table with a volume of Marxist philosophy, pretending to read, but really, looking to see who was available. A moderately attractive brunette with short cropped hair sat two tables away reading an astrology book. I did my usual ploy, approaching the table and asking if I could bum a cigarette. When the girl said okay, I made some comment about astrology, asking what's your sign, or some such nonsense, and the next move I made was asking if it was okay to sit down. The girl nodded her okay, and then one thing led to another, and maybe a half hour into the conversation, all the time being very goal oriented, I asked her if she liked to smoke dope. She said she did. And I said I had some if she wanted to smoke some back at my house, and that we could go together in my car. She enthusiastically nodded her assent. Off we drove back to Kensington in the Red Octopus. Entering the house, I walked up into Stats bedroom attic, where I got a couple of joints. The Statman was eager to offer the joints, and particularly curious about my intentions, especially when he heard that a young lady who was not Delphine was with me. But, as I was not interested in filling in the Statman about my intentions at this time, I simply took the joints and returned downstairs to my room. Rita was waiting there for me. After firing up the j and allowing the cannabis to do its job, a few minutes later, I made my move on her. By this time, Rita was fairly stoned and did not put up any resistance. In fact, she was quite receptive, and the next thing I knew, our clothes came off, and we were fucking. Afterwards, I could feel a measure of guilt, alongside a strange, cold-blooded satisfaction at getting my revenge on Delphine. Not too long after the so-called dirty deed was done, I took Rita back to Berkeley, where I informed her that I was living with someone, and that it was probably not a good idea for us to see each other again. The old pleasure first and honesty after routine. Strangely, she said she understood, and didn't even inquire as to why I had picked her up in the first place. It was almost as if Rita seemed experienced at these one-night stands, or rather, one afternoon stands, and not bothered by it at all. I wondered to myself if Rita had low self-esteem, but preferred thinking she was a liberated woman. The whole thing was sort of easy, but not without its residue of tawdriness and sleaze. And so I had my revenge. What would be the aftermath, I wasn't sure, but what I did know was that things between Delphine and me were not the same. There was now a distance between us that had not existed before, although I had earlier inklings from the Jackson Browne song, which at the time had felt like an emotional bullseye. Still, this business with Kenny, and my subsequent revenge, marked a change. Maybe a lack of trust. Some distance between us, that's for sure. Something. I didn't tell Delphine about my revenge move. It was enough, I told myself, that I had gotten it. I probably enjoyed the edge of moral superiority with her. Whatever it was, I kept it to myself.

CHAPTER 16

Mark is Here (December 1974 – February 1975)

Meanwhile, a couple of weeks prior, Mark, another old time New Rochelle buddy, had arrived. He was freshly divorced from Jane after a marriage of three years, a marriage that went south almost from the start. Mark had no business getting married that young, but had married his high school girlfriend upon hearing of a catastrophic rape that Jane experienced in New York City, coming out of a bar at 2am. When Jane called him that night, she was a physical and emotional mess, and Mark, out of sympathy, and not knowing what else to do, agreed to marry her a month later. Mark knew right from the start that they were incompatible. While Jane was a likeable and upbeat person, she and Mark had different values and life goals. Jane was into money, security, and rising up the career ladder. Mark had no career goals, and was untroubled by this, merely searching for adventure with a desire to travel. Their differences were present right from the start. Ostensibly to save money, they lived with Mark's mother. Probably not a good move for a marriage, but nonetheless a move they made. Mark, a sociology major, also worked at a hospital doing social work. He didn't like it much, while Jane, who had not gone to college, was working her way up the career ladder as a buyer at Bloomingdale's. Things got so bad that by the late fall of 1974, they agreed to an amicable divorce. As they had no property, real assets, or kids, the divorce settlement was simple and fast.

As soon as it was settled, Mark got out of Dodge like a bat out of hell and headed for Berkeley and the coast to see what all the fuss was about, and hang out with me until he got his proverbial land legs. Doug Billips had a room available in North Berkeley and was happy to put Mark up. The two, both of the mellow persuasion, got along really well. As Doug was a recent Berkeley grad, like me, the three of us shared a similar situation. We had no clear idea of a career direction, and none of us were in a hurry to find one. I was probably the most in a hurry of the three of us. I didn't like being called indolent by my dad, and struggled with guilt and embarrassment about being out of work. At least some of the time. Doug and Mark, by contrast, at least on the surface, were not bothered by the lack of career direction at all, and content to just hang out. Though I was starting my second round of acting classes, with no Good Vibes softball, as it was the rainy season, I had less and less to keep me occupied. I was bored. But when the unemployment office contacted me again to do another compulsory job or lose my benefits, the job they offered was a lot less fun than the post office job I had four months earlier. This time it was being a mid-decade census taker in my neighborhood. The job was dreary. I had to go door to door asking a whole bunch of personal questions to get demographic info for the government. The job was tedious, monotonous, and the worst part of it was the contact I had with elderly widows. I discovered firsthand how lonely and isolated people in their late 70s and 80s could be. These ladies, and it was only ladies that I encountered, were so starved for company that they would make me tea, cookies, anything to keep me from leaving. So depressing, and occasionally annoying, it slowed down my route. But I felt duty bound as a human being of the halfway decent variety to stay and listen to their stories of their kids, grandkids, or dead or divorced husbands. In the words of my dead mother, it wouldn't be nice to just up and leave abruptly. In matters of human relations, my mother was rarely if ever less than decent or compassionate, no matter how she felt on the inside, and so I must have learned her lessons well. I stayed and suffered in silence. It didn't help that the pay was the usual $2.30 an hour. Something had to change. It had now been over a year since I'd had any kind of a real job, and the acting class, and hanging out with Doug and Mark or the Statman was getting old. Things with Delphine and I were becoming increasingly distant. Not unpleasant exactly, just more and more surface. This status quo would not hold. The census job ended in mid-February. The unemployment situation was now heading into the homestretch. Pretty soon I would not be able to collect. Low level panic was starting to kick in. What the hell was I gonna do?

CHAPTER 17

The Center Is Not Holding. (March–April 1975)

To pass the time, and there was entirely too much of it, I used waiting for the I ward job pending in Martinez with Stan Mayerson as an excuse and started smoking more pot than at any other time in my life. It was sometimes fun, but when my worry or anxiety was up, it only made things worse. Statman was good company and fun to get stoned with, as was Delphine, one of the few things we still did together, as her time was more and more taken up with her job or her own stained glass work. Convenient ways to avoid contact. I went with it. I didn't push it. Finally, the suspense was killing me, and I contacted Stan Mayerson about the job that had been on hold for six months now. As I called him with bated breath, literally, I was super tense, and could hear in his voice that the news was not good.

"Civil Service won't go for it," he said. "You don't have the requisite two years of work experience, and they won't allow your experience as a patient to substitute for the lack of work in the field.

I'm sorry, because I know you would have made a big contribution working for us. But I don't know what else to say but good luck."

That was it. That dream was over. What was I going to do? I now had two months to get my shit together. Get a job. Any job. Panic was now palpable. But just as strong was my avoidant side. And that side was mostly winning. It was becoming just as easy to get stoned as it was to try to grab the bull by the horns and mobilize myself to look for a job. I didn't really have a clue what I was suited for. I loved the acting classes, but the acting profession persistently maintained a 90% unemployment rate, minimally. A pretty insecure career on a good day. Besides, the sense I was getting from being around actors was that they were overly egotistical, overly concerned with how they looked. I wasn't sure I wanted to spend my life around those kinds of people. So if not acting, then what? I kept coming up empty. The only solace I could take was that I wasn't the only one. Doug was in the same place, and Mark too. Only they weren't twisting in the wind about it. Mark had some leftover savings from his job in the Bronx, and Doug had more time left on his unemployment before panic would set in for him. I was getting more and more worried, bummed, and paralyzed. Luckily, the rainy season ended early, and Dewey softball resumed about six weeks earlier than usual, in mid-February, giving me something to do besides the paltry once-a-week acting classes. At least on weekends. The games took on greater meaning and intensity, given that I had nothing else going on, and I found myself getting more reactive when things didn't go my way on the ball field. Formerly one of the more mellow dudes, I now entered the ranks of the hotheads. I didn't like that, but at the same time I was into the games, and even started pitching, usually the back end of the double headers that we played on both Saturday and Sunday, which increased my emotional investment in the outcomes of games. It brought out my worst side, as when my fielders made mistakes in the field, I frequently got quite upset and yelled at my teammates. Nasty stuff. Statman offered some entertainment and conversational patter, whether stoned or straight. But while fun, it only served as a part time distraction. When the games were over, and I wasn't getting stoned, I would fall back on my worry and low-level panic. Occasionally, and I mean occasionally, I would look at the want ads to see about jobs. But I was glancing at the papers at best, and my fear that I had no job skills or experience caused me to put down the paper and escape into music or reading. Not a good strategy. Time, as it will, was marching on, with not much time left on my unemployment, and yet I was not taking action. Delphine was increasingly busy with her job and stained glass projects, spending more and more time in the basement when not at work, and less and less time with me. And when she was with me, the contact was superficial, even dull. Delphine was not seemingly bothered by it, or if she was, she was not bringing it to my attention. This really started to bother me, and one night towards the end of April, I couldn't take it anymore, and brought up the topic of our relationship, and my unemployment. Delphine tried to be supportive and encouraging about my work situation, but was kind of detached. Then, I said our relationship seemed increasingly off track. Sex was more and more infrequent, and our intimate conversations happened less and less. She didn't disagree, but was not that perturbed by the state of affairs. I told her I needed more, and was worried that things would fall apart unless we put effort and energy into making it better. I suggested a camping trip up in Mendocino County, near Fort Bragg, thinking that camping had been a glue when we first fell in love, so it was my hope that it could be again. She agreed, and in the beginning of May, we went off together to reignite our love flame. Delphine, besides our bringing the basic camping equipment, sleeping bags, tent, cooking utensils, and food, brought her jazz music book - *Blues People* by Leroy Jones - which I had read earlier that year, a masterful description of the uniquely Black art form, while I brought a copy of *The Maltese Falcon*, which I was preparing to present to my acting class as a kind of mini one-man show, with me playing the Bogart part, the Peter Lorre part, and the Mary Astor part. I was ambitious (grandiose?), and unskilled at acting techniques, but undaunted. It was one of the few things in my life giving me any pleasure, and so I was going for the gusto, as they said in the Schlitz commercial.

The weekend started fine. We made love on the beach near Fort Bragg and the town of Mendocino. But from there, things deteriorated. The more time went on during the weekend, the more I began to see that the lyrics to the song "Late for the Sky" were coming true right before my eyes. Delphine seemed like a stranger to me. We really didn't understand each other, or communicate very well. Delphine had less and less tolerance for my gloomy outlook and constant obsessing about a job which I was not really pursuing. She said that I needed to stop worrying, and start doing. In my vulnerable state, while recognizing she was right, I felt attacked and uncared for. A bad mix. Delphine was on her way in her own career, and needed someone who had his shit together to go along with her as a partner on her journey. She was confident and motivated. I was in bad shape, and getting worse. The weekend proved to be a disaster. We left Mendocino both feeling completely alone. It marked the beginning of the end.

CHAPTER 18

The Beginning of the End, or the End of the Beginning (May–July 1975)

Back in Kensington, a month or less before unemployment ran out, I still wasn't taking any active steps to pursue work. The only consistencies in my life were the acting class and Dewey softball. I spent more and more time smoking pot and snorting coke, which I'd just started to do with more regularity. I was escaping, not able to get myself in tow. As the month went on, Delphine and I were together less and less, and not even having sex anymore. We barely talked, other than surface politeness. One weekend, she left to attend a stained glass workshop in Santa Cruz, leaving just Statman and me. Ben, the other housemate, was never around, spending his off-work hours with his girlfriend. Statman had broken it off with Erin, his girlfriend of six months, who had been a regular presence around the Kensington house, and he was now embarking on what he called a fuckathon. He invited over a girl named Erica, who he had recently been schtupping, along with her friend Melanie, for what he hoped would be a ménage, if I was interested, which he knew I was, given my deteriorated status with Delphine. That Saturday night they came over for many lines of coke and a barbecue. Not in that order. Melanie and Erica were both waitresses at Olegs, a restaurant in Berkeley, and they were up for anything. Friendly, frisky, and sexy, with the coke igniting our libidos after a few lines, the four of us got down to business in Statman's bed. First, Erica with Stat, and Melanie with me, and then we switched. Having done enough experimenting in homo-erotic land, my curiosity was sated, and I was not interested, nor did I sense any interest from Stat, in closing that sexual loop. We were all in hog heaven. I felt minimal to no guilt about fooling around on Delphine. The handwriting was on the wall. It was all over but the shouting. But I would not be broadcasting my activities either. That would be bad form. It was fucking fun, but it was merely another temporary diversion from the matter at hand, which was getting a fucking job! Melanie and Erica were both hot, fun, and sweet in their way, but only momentarily did they take away the anxiety. The clock was ticking, only two more weeks until unemployment was running out. Things were falling apart on all fronts.

Following Delphine's return from Santa Cruz, she and I sat down to talk about us.

I said, "This is no good. I'm not getting the support I need. It's not your fault. We're going in too different directions. You've got your career path and I'm still trying to figure out mine. I still love you but I need more."

"This sucks," said Delphine . "I love you too, but we're not helping each other. I need someone who has got their shit together and you're still trying to get yours together. Unfortunately, I think you're right. You're a great guy but it's just not happening anymore. I think we should separate and just be friends."

"Yeah, I think I need to be by myself and figure it out on my own."

In other words, we both realized that the relationship wasn't working out. Delphine said we were moving in different directions, which was her nice way of saying that her life was moving forward and mine was going backward. We agreed to both move out in a month, on July 1. It would have been untenable financially for me to stay living with Statman, so we both gave Stat notice. He understood, but was not happy, as we were fun tenants and we all basically got along, and it would be a hassle for him to find new roommates as congenial, but that was that. Delphine and I tried to be civil to each other in that last month together. She was gone a lot, looking for a place to live, while I was really starting to panic, but trying to gather my forces. In desperation, I went to my father, which I hated. Telling him of my plight, humiliated, I asked for some money to tide me over until I found work. He was pissed, wondering what the hell I'd been doing all this time on unemployment, twiddling my thumbs. In angry tones, he voiced that maybe it would be better if I fended for myself to teach me a lesson. This only succeeded in pissing me off, and I slammed the receiver down. Equal parts frightened and pissed, I galvanized myself into applying for four busboy and dishwashing jobs in one day, which was also humiliating, but at least I was doing something real. The next day, in what I could only imagine as my father's guilt and terror at the thought of me being homeless, he agreed to bankroll me for the next two months, but said that would be it. This was a life raft on a sinking ship. I promptly combed the Co-Op bulletin board, and found some rooms to rent in the Berkeley hills available July 1. One lovely, kind, elderly woman in her mid 70s, a widow with grown children, seemed to take a liking to me, and somehow was able to look past my obvious desperation. I don't know what her trip was, maybe she saw another opportunity to parent another kid. I don't know but she agreed to rent to me. The rate was a reasonable $175 a month. Thank God. One less thing to worry about for the time being. Delphine found a place to live in South Berkeley, not too far from where Patty Hearst had been kidnapped a year or so earlier, near UC campus, with two guys and one other girl. We managed to retain our politeness with each other.

Relieved that I wasn't going to be homeless, by Dad's temporary reprieve, I relaxed my desperate job search, thinking that I would wait until I moved into my new digs, which freed me up to continue getting stoned and coked out with Statman until I moved. At a gathering at Bill Cody's and Muff's house in San Rafael, my old DJ friend was having a get-together to celebrate getting full time work at his radio station. It was unusual for me to be so relaxed, probably from the relief of the pressure and worry of running out of money, so I was more available to just have fun. There were more OSU people there, some of whom I didn't know, including a very attractive brunette who was soon to be married, in just two weeks, but was at the party by herself. As was the ritual with my crowd, besides the pot luck and barbecue, there was the requisite getting stoned and sitting on the floor listening to music. The soon to be married lady was Emma. Originally a New Jersey girl, and now living in San Anselmo, she was vibing me most of the night, as if to say she was interested and available. It was weird, and certainly unclear. But as the party wound down, Emma said she was too stoned to drive, and was told emphatically by Muff that she should crash at their place for the night. By this time, there were only four or five people there, leaving Emma and me to our own devices. Pretty soon, the last few folks left, and Cody and Muff went to bed. Almost immediately, Emma and I started making out, then proceeded quickly to the room she would be staying in. Emma would voice guilt, but her ardor easily overcame the guilt, and like a match to crinkled paper we were off to the races. Super intense. We woke up around ten the next day, and spent the afternoon with Muff, driving around Marin. Muff was incredibly non-judgmental about her friend's behavior as she functioned as chauffeur to our backseat high school make-out antics. Wild, crazy, and weird. But I had no objections. After all, I didn't know her husband-to-be. That was her problem, and her choice, I said to myself. And so it didn't bother me the least. The excitement of it all easily overcame any qualms I might have had or should have had. By the end of the day, Emma's guilt took over, and we said our goodbyes, never to see one another again. Such were the times. Such were my times.

CHAPTER 19

Transition of Failure (July 1975)

July came pretty fast. My sexual respite was once again only a temporary diversion as the reality of my life came rushing back almost immediately. With Delphine and I separating and departing into new living spaces, and me saying adios from living with my doppelgänger friend the Statman, I was alone, maybe for the first time ever. Living alone in the Berkeley hills by myself in a strange person's house. With no work, and Dad's gifted money to tide me over for the next couple of months, and all the guilt and shame associated with this renewed dependency, things were not good. Living alone felt weird, uncomfortable. I was used to living with other people my age, or with a woman.

Now, neither. I was not in good shape. The old restlessness, agitation, and difficulty sleeping took over again. I was too fucked up to concentrate, or look for work, or be able to present myself normally. I was even missing Carole, really, for the first time in months. Really messed up. Luckily, while I was in Brennan's, a local bar by the Berkeley pier, I ran into Statman's former girlfriend Erin, who I knew a little. Immediately upon sitting down with me, she sensed something was wrong. A nurse, and street-smart lady from Brooklyn, she was not easily fooled by pretense, and expressed concern. I filled her in on my situation, and she was saddened but not surprised to hear Delphine and I were history, always thinking we weren't well suited. But she could see that I was speed rapping and going in and out of making sense, going off on tangents. Agitated. At times hilariously funny, but obviously unstable. Erin became my lifeline for the next month. One of my worst months ever. Erin, an RN, was also in transition. She had been a nurse for seven years now, and had burnt out on the work, and she too was betwixt and between, also collecting unemployment while trying to figure out what she wanted to do. She had time on her hands, and luckily for me, she took a liking to me. We kind of naturally hit it off, so for the next month she became my best friend, or maybe I should say a kind of nursemaid. I was still a mess. Sleeping poorly, pacing, unable to stay focused and persistently getting off topic, I was a handful. A saving grace for Erin was that I could be entertaining in my manic craziness. Erin and I laughed a lot. We got super close, but we did not sleep together. Erin and I both realized it would have been a disaster, less for her and more for me, but for her as well. It was the last thing I needed at this point. I needed a friend. Even I was capable of realizing this, despite my crazy state. So even though I stayed over at her apartment a few times, even once or twice with her in her bed, we never messed around. Erin and I must have spent hours together daily. I think she was thinking that if she hung in there with me, she could maybe help me get my act together. It was a noble effort. But after a week or two of this, she realized that being with me was heavy lifting, and suggested that I find a therapist, which I hadn't had now for almost three years, since my last hospitalization back in Columbus, and the year after while Carole and I lived together.

Erin's next-door neighbor was a shrink in town, and gave her some names. I told Erin I wanted a female therapist. I had never had one, and thought it might be helpful to me, given that I had had my own difficulties with women in the past, and maybe would offer more of a nurturing presence. I met with a young, thirty-something, very attractive brunette psychologist. We connected. But one aspect of my state was hyper-sexuality, so the sessions were kind of disjointed. I think I was more interested in trying to seduce Joan, the therapist, than get the help I needed. Joan, not completely inexperienced, but not that seasoned either, while extremely nice and caring, was in over her head. I was too much for her, and I resisted her entreaties to get on medication. I was done with that, I told her adamantly, but despite my negativity towards meds, I wasn't sleeping well, really not doing better. Also, despite my father's temporary financial reprieve, I was getting more and more fragmented, tangential, and really struggling just to take care of myself on any basic level. Easily flying off the handle. It was miserable, but my agitated state kept me from feeling how awful I truly felt. Things were getting worse. Three weeks into the move into the room in the Berkeley hills, and with Erin's assistance, I threw in the towel and decided to admit myself into the psych hospital in Berkeley, Herrick Hospital. Another defeat. But strangely, during the intake at the emergency room at Herrick, when the worker asked me if I was hearing voices, even though I wasn't, I said yes. I think I was worried that they wouldn't admit me if I said no. I knew that in Berkeley, because there were so many wackos walking around, you had to be REALLY fucked up to get admitted into the nut house.

Anyway, upon hearing that I was hearing voices, the nurses must have thought I was really fucked up, and needed more controls, so they admitted me to the locked unit. This was new for me, except for the week I had spent in a locked unit all the way back in 1968, when I had set a fire, out of boredom, during my first hospitalization at the Institute of Living, following my first breakdown. Here I was, seven years later, at age twenty-five, experiencing my fifth hospitalization, with no career and three romantic relationships down the tubes. Nowheresville.

Herrick Hospital 3 West Locked Facility

Fucking fucked up. But as fucked up as I was, there was one arena I was a pro, and that was in dealing with the shrinks, the nuts, and the nurses in a looney bin. Even in a locked unit. All it meant was more staff and less freedom. I could do that. I had strange confidence about my abilities here in this regard. It must be like what repeat offenders in jail feel. Like the most comfort in their lives is in jail. A grizzly thought, but true. I immediately became attached to a sweet, pretty, warm Black woman, slightly older than me, named Pearl. When you're in the nuthouse, one of the good things is your guard drops, and you can be yourself, completely, warts and all. I think I liked that aspect. And I think some of the other patients did too. Pearl and I were completely honest with each other. She was in a rocky, abusive relationship with a boyfriend, had two young kids, aged five and three, and had gotten completely overwhelmed and thought about killing herself. Luckily, her mother had the sense to get her admitted to Herrick, and even Pearl had to admit to herself that she was in over her head. Upon entering Herrick, she immediately relaxed and began the process of trying to pick up the pieces of her life. To regain the strength to resume her parenting, find work, and deal with her abusive boyfriend. Hanging out with Pearl, mostly at night, gave me respite from the craziness on the unit, not to mention my own craziness, which was not abating despite the Haldol antipsychotic they were giving me. I hated those things, and as a veteran of looney bins, had long learned how to cheek the meds. I did my own brand of dosing, taking the stuff once a day and cheeking them the other two times the nurses handed them out. But whatever I was doing was not helping. I was still agitated as hell. Dr. Feld, an asshole psychiatrist, about as unempathetic as they come, was very impatient with my lack of progress. When Erin came to visit, he told her that he was not encouraged, and if I didn't progress, and progress soon, they were going to have to place me in the state hospital. Napa State. Erin, naturally alarmed, met with me about ten days into my stay to relay the news from Dr. Warmth. What would be my recourse? Well, there were some. There were half-way houses in the community, which I had some familiarity with, having worked in a quarter way house at Rose Lane upon moving to Berkeley. Following some fast research, Erin found three for me to investigate. Two were in Berkeley and one out in Concord, a suburb about twenty-five minutes from Berkeley, near where I had done relief work a couple of years earlier. Berkeley Place, Bonita House and Phoenix House. First stop: Berkeley Place. Erin took me there in her blue VW bug, waiting for me while I checked the place out and had an interview. Upon entering, I was greeted by a staff counselor about my age who began to show me around. Then, distracted by the chaos in the place, which included near fights, and the common rooms in disarray, a very attractive brunette, maybe nineteen years old, began following us. As the counselor's distraction continued, he finally said, "Why doesn't Katy show you around."

Well show me around she did, right to her bedroom, where she started kissing and hugging me, going for my genitals with her hands.

0-60 in five seconds, almost literally. I didn't object, believe me, but I must admit I was dazzled and flummoxed by the situation. After about five minutes of this, the counselor seemed to find us, as if these situations with new potential residents and Katy weren't a new thing, and quickly maneuvered me into the staff office for an interview. The counselor was clearly in over his head. He seemed stressed and anxious, and his questions were scattershot. Way too chaotic and unstructured. I could tell the counselor was looking to fill beds, but besides the allure of Katy, which was a lot, the place did not feel like a place where I could get my proverbial shit together.

The next place, Bonita House, had the same feel without the benefit of Katy. Chaotic, disheveled, and disorganized. I was getting worried. Finally, about two days before Napa State hospital time, I went to Concord to visit the third and final halfway house. Phoenix House. I entered into what immediately felt was a calmer vibe. A guy named Tim greeted me and ushered me into a very tight office space where two other staff people were already seated. A Black woman in her late twenties, and Will, the clinical director, who looked to be in his late thirties. I sat on a funky lazy boy chair, perched on the arm rest. I was hyped up. When they asked me why I was there, and what I thought my problems were, I went into the Jackson Browne song that had been so prescient in my relationship with Delphine before we broke up. I sang the whole song to the three staff people. On key, too. They seemed to like it. They all seemed nice. Not stupid, not afraid, and not smug. They told me that I was in, barring any mishaps or changes of mind on my part after I spent an overnight at the house. I liked the vibe at Phoenix much better than the other two places. Even though Phoenix didn't have a crazy Katy around to escort me into her room for sex, no questions asked, what it did have was a sense of calm, and structure, and organization. I liked how the staff interacted with the sixteen residents, both men and women, almost all between the ages of eighteen and thirty. Yes, Phoenix was for me. And with an uneventful overnight, mellow you might say, I was in, beating the transfer to Napa State hospital by a day, which might have been it for me. People who went to Napa stayed a long time, and most of them didn't get better.

I felt like I had my best shot here at Phoenix and I took it. Erin dropped me off, after arranging things with my landlady up in the hills, and also getting the social workers at Herrick to initiate the social security process, so I could pay for my stay at Phoenix and be eligible for Medi-Cal.

CHAPTER 20

Rising from the Ashes: Phoenix House (August 1975)

On August 6, 1975, after my friend Erin dropped me off, I was now out of Berkeley and in Concord, a resident. I must say that just because the Phoenix place was calmer, more organized, and structured than the other two places doesn't mean it wasn't crazy at times. After all, it was populated by crazy people, who go off from time to time. I was assigned a counselor, Tim, who was at the house for one twenty-four hour shift, and one twelve hour shift a week. The rest of the time, there were other counselors on duty. The other counselors were assigned other residents to work with. A total of seven full time counselors each did one overnight a week, sleeping in one of the three houses on the campus. There was a step system to the three houses: the Main House, the Far Out House and the Green House. The Main House, where the newest and least together residents lived, housed eight people. Two people shared four rooms. Residents were assigned cooking, dish washing and room cleaning responsibilities. While many patients were prescribed medications, like antipsychotics, mood stabilizers and antidepressants, the staff attitude was if residents didn't want to take the meds, that was on us. It was all voluntary. In fact, if anything, the staff vibe around medications seemed to be slightly discouraging. The staff believed more in counseling. Individual and group counseling. There was a day program called Phoenix Center, which consisted of numerous groups, some therapeutic, that residents were required to attend unless they were in school or working at a job. Occasionally, resident's families would come to the house for family therapy sessions, but that was infrequent. Mostly, it was milieu therapy. The environment of the place, physical and social, was supposed to be the primary healing force.

The program structure was designed to give residents room and space, autonomy and responsibility, in order to maximize healing. Unlike the hospital structure, which was hierarchical and controlling, the halfway house structure was designed to treat residents as equal partners in their healing, with as much say in the running of the house as they could take on. Counselor - resident interactions were supposed to be as egalitarian as possible. When a resident had been in the program for a while, and there was mutual agreement, then the resident was promoted from the Main House to the Far Out House, where there would be less staff around, more freedom, except at night, when the staff person doing their twenty-four hour shift would sleep there. Much more freedom, and much less supervision. I was happy to be here. As happy as a mental patient could be in a mental health facility. If I had to be somewhere, this was it. Tim, my counselor, was a regular, down-to-earth guy. A recent graduate of UC Berkeley, with a psych major, he frequently came to his shift with his dog, Guthrie, who he was sharing with his live-in girlfriend, Kelly Anne. Tim and I would hang out, sometimes completing our sessions while playing 1-on-1 basketball. He was quite good, taller than me, and had some good moves. But mostly our meetings were in the office. Tim laughed easily, and seemed to have a natural appreciation for my quirkiness, which made relating easy and fun.

When he was off his shifts, there were plenty of other interesting counselors around. There were two in particular I liked, who I called the Jewish contingent, Devin and Joani. Devin was someone I knew from Dewey softball. A rival player on one of the other recreation league teams, we had socialized together at parties. Devin was a very good-looking guy, smart, and a very good ball player. Good sense of humor. Devin had a VERY good-looking girlfriend, Ellen, who occasionally dropped by while he was working. Devin and I struck up a very quick and tight connection. Both competitive athletes, we got into it at the ping pong table, where we would play tight games, with Devin throwing periodic wisecrack insults at me, which I returned in kind. It was fun, and felt like these counselors were more friends than counselors, making for a very congenial atmosphere. Then there was Joani . A dark-haired beauty. Jewish, smart, sweet, attached to her boyfriend, and a good athlete, who I immediately fell headlong in love with. She was easy to talk with, and heading for a career in psychology. I looked forward to the shifts with Devin and Joani as much as I did when Tim was on. The four other regular counselors, Tom, Bob, Edie, and Lanette, were great too. They all seemed to have this easy, natural way of relating which made me feel instantly accepted, but not in a phony way. I'm not sure how the other residents felt. I felt kind of different from the other residents, mostly anyway. Maybe because I shared a similar background with the counselors. Shared similar intellectual and cultural interests, as I had really come from their bougie, bohemian world, so it was easy for me to relate. I can't say it was because I was less fucked up. Maybe in some ways. The house had its usual smattering of schizophrenics, manic-depressives and severe depressives, but here, diagnosis wasn't really stressed.

What counted was the relationship counselors and residents formed, and functionality, with a stress on the practical steps necessary for independence. I never felt like a specimen, always a person, which for me, led to good vibes in general. But I do not want to create the impression that all was rosy, all the time. Afterall, it was a psychiatric halfway house, designed to keep people out of the hospital, or more often, to help people make the transition from being a hospital patient back into independent functioning in the community. As such, we fucked up people could be rather intense at times.

Phoenix was a community program, and not an institution, as such. It aspired to create as homelike an atmosphere as possible. Because the staff and the director Will saw themselves as progressive, and permitted sexual relations between the residents, they also decided to experiment with allowing residents to drink alcohol on weekends. This experiment in maximizing normality just so happened to start the first couple of weeks I was at the house, and had recently been voted on by the residents at a house meeting. In other words, residents had some say in the running of the program, and at least when I arrived, staff was bending over backwards to give residents their say. In my progressive mindset, I thought this was great, in theory. In practice, I'm not sure it worked out so well. Living in the house were some male residents who could get rather aggressive without booze. One resident in particular, a guy named Larry, was from a white, working class background, and had grown up in a hardscrabble, drug addled working class town, Richmond, next to Berkeley. Larry was an edgy guy on a good day. He and I were friendly, but also had an edgy, competitive way of bantering and relating. Larry had been psychotic, but also had a significant crank habit. Methamphetamine. I don't think he was using while he was at Phoenix, but I can't be sure. Anyway, on one of the first drinking nights, Larry had a few beers, enough to make his edginess erupt into downright challenging rowdiness. He had a hankering for one of the female residents, a resident that I was not interested in, but on this night, Larry misinterpreted my friendliness to this Clara person as coming on to her. With three drinks and maybe some crank in him, Larry's usual humorous banter switched. He came at me with very vocal aggressive posturing, as if he was ready to fight. Larry was maybe a hundred and thirty pounds, and shorter than me, but wiry, and maybe more experienced at fighting than me, which was not saying much. I was not intimidated, but neither was I into fighting. It got very tense before Tim, who was on duty that night, and taller and stronger than the both of us, intervened. That night, there were other close calls between other male residents. The female residents were no better. When they drank, their sexual, and dare I say aggressive, inhibitions dropped. Not a good thing, because the jealousy and envy it produced was pretty ugly. A recipe for mayhem. After this Saturday night debacle, which luckily resulted in no violence, marked the end of that progressive experiment, I was glad. I didn't need that kind of intensity. I had enough intensity inside my head, and I suspected that others did too. We didn't need to add to it. If I wanted to drink, I could always go to a bar. It was allowed, and sometimes I would. As much as I liked the fact that the Phoenix people were willing to experiment, and treat us like regular human beings, the drinking thing was really a bridge too far. The fact was, we were there because we were mentally unstable, and a calm sense of order and structure were not such a bad thing. Actually, therapeutic. The staff, seeing that it was a mistake, went back to a no drinking rule on the three house campus. It was the worst program gaffe committed while I was there. I needed structure and calm. I knew that much about myself. I did not need the excitement of a rowdy barroom. Getting my head together, feeling better, and being more functional were my most important goals, and despite this honest mistake with the drinking, I saw that Phoenix House and the Day Center would be my best shot at mental health. Maybe my last shot. I was hell bent on making the most of the opportunity. I was told I could stay up to two years if I needed to. With my SSI being awarded, and my MediCal coming in, I had a way to pay for the room and board and meds if I needed them. The long length of stay, if I wanted to use it, made for a much more relaxed atmosphere. At least for me. For some of the other residents, I'm not so sure. Some used it to languish and stagnate. I saw myself as different. With the exception of Clara, I was clearly the most intellectual of the residents, and along with her the most motivated.

CHAPTER 21

The Clinical Director

Will was the clinical director. A Harvard graduate in English, he had attended Cooper Union, studying art, moved to California, became ordained as an Episcopal minister, and now one year out, was a graduate of CSPP, a free standing graduate clinical psychology program in Berkeley. Will was bright, kind, and open. Pretty versatile resume. He laughed easily and was not intimidated by craziness. He had a calm demeanor. Tim suggested, as he could see that I was motivated, that I start having regular sessions with Will in addition to the time with him. Will had recently gotten his psychology license, but was full time here at Phoenix. He considered himself a Rogerian. This meant he was very client-centered, very accepting of the client's experience. A few weeks into my stay, Will and I met twice a week at the house, or on walks. Instead of getting alarmed at the often weird, provocative things I could say, Will would laugh. I think he thought some of the things I was saying were absurd, but funny. I had a style or a pose of presenting myself like a tough guy. Fashioned after Humphrey Bogart, an actor who had been my first culture hero as a teenager, it was my way of pretending I was not vulnerable. Will saw through this right away. But he did it in a nice way. He laughed as if he found it amusing, yet ridiculous. I must admit, I couldn't disagree. It may have hurt if Will had been more heavy-handed. But his way of calling me out on my ridiculous pose made it possible for me to laugh at myself as well. In other words, Will was saying to me, "You're not Bogart, but just as scared and vulnerable as the next guy, and it's ok that you're that way. I still like and love you and care about you." At the same time, Will was saying that if I needed the Bogart pose, well that was ok too. Everything was ok. This kind of acceptance, and recognition about parts of who I was, and who I had created for self-protection was a tonic for me. This unconditional positive regard stuff was real, and it could work, particularly if it allowed me to be seen in all my various guises and intensities.

Will also had a certain charisma with the counseling staff. It was apparent. They looked up to him. They admired his intelligence and his openness and kindness. If he erred, as we all do, he erred on the side of looseness, or over-permissiveness. As was revealed to me by Devin and Joani, who could both be kind of gossipy about staff, there was a lot of incestuous sex stirring between staff counselors. Edie, a very sexy, poetic, literary sort, was fooling around with Bob, a fledgling filmmaker, who saw the job at Phoenix as a way station towards a career as a movie director, but was doing little about it. Because the boundaries at the house were kind of loose, residents knew a lot about what was going on with staff, which really made the place feel like a family. I ate it up like a starving thirsty beast after years of famine in the Gobi Desert. During the day, there was a whole other world to get involved in. Phoenix Center, the community day treatment program, ran with its own set of counselors and staff, and was where the boss of the place, executive director Nik McDonough, worked. One of the requirements of being a resident at Phoenix house was that all of the residents had to be out of the house between 10 and 3. Either in school (usually Diablo Valley, the local community college), at a job, or at Phoenix center. Most residents didn't work or go to school, so I came to Phoenix Center with the other residents during the day.

Phoenix Center was run by a spunky but sweet Texan named Micky, a divorcee with a masters in psychology who also had a superb natural way of relating to us crazies. Micky ran a nice program. It consisted of a daily check-in meeting, a yoga or stretching class, lunch, and in the afternoons, a vocational group to help people figure out work or career related issues, and an art group, either drawing, or learning how to airbrush t-shirts. Additionally, once a week, a psychology grad student at the Transpersonal Psychology Program in Palo Alto would come and run a group on astrology and understanding your horoscope. All very hippie-dippy and countercultural. Perfect for my ilk, and really, a lot of the center clients, some of whom didn't live at Phoenix House. Those people usually were ex-residents, now living independently in the town of Concord, or in satellite housing, a type of living situation where ex psych patients would live by themselves or with other residents with a minimum of counselor intervention by Phoenix staff. Maybe once a week, staff would come to run a meeting, and be on call if crises came up. So the center had current and usually former Phoenix house people in attendance. Most had a prior relationship to Phoenix before getting involved with Phoenix Center.

Every fall and spring, the center would take people on a camping trip. A month after I arrived, there was a weekend camping trip to Mendocino which I participated in with Micky, two other center counselors, and fifteen other clients. As I had only been to Mendocino once (during the failed last-ditch effort to save my relationship with Delphine), this was an opportunity to enjoy the beauty of Mendocino under less desperate, albeit still crazy, conditions. And although I was frequently still agitated, prone to going off on verbal tangents, and occasionally losing touch with what was going on in front of me, I was still able to tune into the beauty of the hills and redwood forests that surrounded us at our campground. Micky and Dave, the Phoenix Center counselors, were really easy going. Particularly Micky. With that Texas southern drawl, she gave off a very accepting vibe, and was easy to talk to. She let us in on what was going on in her life, which I really liked. Micky had been married to an abusive, alcoholic man back in Texas, and had come to the Bay Area in part to escape him and what she called the redneck ways of west Texas. Her favorite expression when talking about people and relationships was, "You gotta set your limits," a lesson that I guess Micky had learned the hard way after dealing with an abusive drunk. But it was an expression that I had never heard before. As I was getting adjusted to the program, one of the things that I was picking up was the psychological jargon bandied about by the staff. *Set your limits* was a biggie. Be assertive, don't let anybody walk all over you. Say what you need. This was relevant in general, but of particular use with my crowd of crazies. Another biggie, expression-wise, was, "Push your buttons," an updated version of allowing someone to cause you to react due to you having a particular issue. Again, of particular relevance for us. Maybe we crazies had more buttons to push, or our reactions when our buttons were pushed were more extreme. I think a bit of both. Anyway, the staff psychological jargon trickled down, and became part of the lingo that residents used with each other when interacting. The jargon was everywhere, part of the culture of the place. And I was settling in with both the house staff and center staff. It was homey and made me feel comfortable when I wasn't thinking about my problems: what I was gonna do with my life, my three major breakups, and generally wondering what was wrong with me. I guess that was the main one that caused my failures, although Will and the rest of the staff would not have called these failures, but challenges or difficulties. All the negative stuff I could think or say had a positive reframe, and while I was initially embarrassed by calling my failures a difficulty or challenge (it felt like bullshit at first), I began to get used to it, and started to see it as part of my reprogramming. In a good way, mostly. I wasn't quite sure, but I was starting to get used to the idea that maybe I wasn't such a bad guy.

Back at the house, a month into my stay, I was feeling comfortable. Comfortable enough to try to see if I could work. I looked in the help wanted ads, and saw a job at a place called New York Deli in Walnut Creek, a couple of towns over from Concord. They were looking for a dishwasher. As I had been a dishwasher at IHOP a few years back in my student days, I figured I could do it. They hired me, and I got the feeling that they liked me, so I started a forty-hour gig, five days a week. I told my bosses I was living in Concord, but didn't mention I was living in a halfway house for fear that they would discriminate against me, or pity me, neither of which would have been good. So I played it close to the vest. The job lasted two weeks. My focus sucked. I was so hyper chatty with the waitresses and occasionally the customers that I frequently got behind on the dishwashing and the quality of my dishwashing was below par. In the words of the Phoenix staff, I was having challenges. That's not how it felt to me, particularly when I got let go. But ultimately what it meant was I wasn't ready to go back to work. I was still fucked up. Challenges, failures, however you wanted to talk about it, I couldn't do a fucking dishwasher job. It was demoralizing, but in the spirit of Phoenix, I tried not being too hard on myself. It wasn't easy. But it was also true that I wasn't that stable. While I had brought antipsychotic medication (Haldol) with me, mostly to calm me down and help me sleep, I rarely used it. Only when I had been up more than two nights in a row did I consider it. And when I took the stuff, it was only because I was so on the blink from not sleeping that I didn't know what else to do. I wasn't getting much exercise, unless you count weekly 1-on-1 basketball with Tim, or weekly ping pong with Devin. I was smoking a pack-and-a-half a day, and had been since age fifteen. The problem was, as the evening wore on, I generally got more stimulated, which made it hard to get shuteye, so at my worst, I took the Haldol, which worked like a sledgehammer, knocking me out, dead to the world, only to wake up pretty groggy and spacey in the morning. I took it as little as possible, and the staff did not make an issue of it, as their philosophy was very anti-medical. But not so anti that they couldn't see some value in medications as a mode of very last resort. They weren't Langians who ran their residential programs without having their residents use medications. Their philosophy was that medications interfered with the natural healing process each individual possessed, including people who were experiencing psychosis. Phoenix people were less doctrinaire, more flexible, but clearly more in the Langian camp than the medical model camp. Phoenix's philosophy seemed just right for me, although I was intrigued with a therapeutic community devoted to allowing people to go through their psychotic experiences without interference by medications. From what I read and heard about from the staff at Phoenix, the jury was out about the Langian method. Too many people stayed crazy, and far fewer were able to process through their psychotic experiences completely organically. Despite one of my many poses, I was finding out I wasn't as all-or-nothing radical as I had pretended, not just about politics, but in just about all realms. The absolutist view was the path of fanatics and fundamentalists, and that just wasn't my bag, though in my confusion, sometimes I mistook my provocative poses for how I really felt about things. I just really got off on baiting people, particularly my father, but really anyone who I perceived to be part of the mainstream establishment. It was fun to do, but push come to shove, I really didn't believe a lot of the bullshit I said, and still could dish out. This is one of the things I was learning from Will, and the place as a whole.

CHAPTER 22

Hijinx and Hoosegow

Residency wise, I progressed quickly enough that by six weeks into my stay, in late September, a room opened up, and I was promoted to the Far Out House, fifty paces or so from the main house, where four residents lived, and where counseling staff slept during their overnight stays. Of course, there was always someone on duty. The night watchman at the main house, usually a college student, came on at 10pm, and stayed until 8, when the counselor woke up for their shift exchange meeting, to discuss any events or situations that may have occurred, and to read the log, the staff communication vehicle.

In the Far Out House, there was one girl, Tina, who was really the only person amongst the residents that I could really relate to. The other residents, while mostly fine in their way, I didn't really connect with that much. Tina was a college graduate, somewhat intellectual, read a lot and was on the hippie-dippy end of things. While somewhat unattractive physically, we had good rapport, and one night, we got it on just to see what it would be like. It was not that hot, in both senses of the word so Tina and I both decided it would be best if we just stayed friends, which we were somehow able to do. Tina had had a couple of serious depressions, and an overdose, from which she nearly died, so she too had logged her units as a mental patient in a nuthouse before coming to Phoenix. She came from a middle-class background in nearby Walnut Creek, a bougie suburb of the corporate variety. Her parents, while smart, were very mainstream, and Tina in her bookish way, rebelled from this alienated and cramped way of growing up. She graduated from UC Santa Cruz, a pretty hippie school, which led her to pot, acid, a bad romance, and your basic heavy depression and suicide attempt. I enjoyed the glib way Tina talked about her life, making her easy to talk to and listen to. If she were more physically attractive, she could have made a good partner. As it was, while at the Far Out House, we became good friends.

In one of my more up states, after the one-and-done sexual encounter with Tina, I decided to get off the Phoenix compound and look for bigger bear. I went by myself to a local bar populated by twenty and thirty-year-olds, and as I was in a more loquacious phase, was able to talk up a pretty blonde sitting at the bar. She somehow took a liking to me, and somewhat tipsy, accepted my offer to come back to the Far Out House. I liked that she wasn't put off by where I was living, as she didn't think I seemed particularly nuts, and besides, was intrigued by the communal situation. When we arrived back at the Far Out House, nobody was there, making it easier and more private for us to do our business. The blonde was cool, but for some reason, after that night I felt no desire to get together with her again. And so that was that. But the experience at the bar made me feel like I wanted to be off the Phoenix campus more often. Sometimes, in the middle of the night, particularly when I wasn't feeling too stable or confident that I could drive, I walked to the 7/11, about a half a mile away.

One night, a couple of weeks after the blonde bar pick-up, I was walking home after purchasing a pack of Viceroys and a couple of Snickers bars, and a Concord city cop stopped me. I didn't know why. I was shocked. I wasn't doing anything wrong. I didn't think it was illegal to walk alone in the middle of the night on a main drag. But apparently the Concord cops thought differently. They stopped me while they checked on my priors. Much to my surprise, after doing their search, they informed me that I owed $150.00 in parking tickets. They put me in handcuffs and I spent the night alone in a cell. The cops must have been bored or something. The next morning, they allowed me one phone call, and I called Phoenix, and Tim came to the police station and brought the $150 to bail me out. Luckily, I was no stranger to jail, having spent a night there in Columbus during the riots, so I wasn't that freaked out about it. The counselors coming to my aid with the bailout money only increased my attachment to the place, to the staff, and to Tim in particular, and increased my desire to get better. But the experience reinforced something else. As I was walking down the street that night after returning from the 7/11, I remember thinking to myself, God I really feel relaxed. This is nice. This is what it feels like to feel good, and the very next second the cops were rousting me from out of nowhere. It's as if the universe got a whiff that I was starting to relax, to feel good, and it was reminding me *DON'T EVER LET DOWN YOUR GUARD. The world is a dangerous place motherfucker, you got to be prepared, be ready for anything sucker.* A cosmic lesson. Disappointing, but perhaps a truth about life. I never went out by myself again in the middle of the night. Always took my car. The world was a weird place.

CHAPTER 23

Dad Visits, Meets Will

A couple of months before Thanksgiving, I was fully invested in my life at Phoenix. I was very connected to the staff, and sensed that they took a special liking to me, as I was like one of them, therefore easiest to relate to. Maybe I was a cautionary tale to them that this could happen to anybody, if it happened to someone like them. Also, I was pretty engaging and looked for common points of interest with all of the staff. With Bob and Edie, I shared an interest in film, theater and acting. With Tim, I discussed Bob Dylan and Bruce Springsteen, whose breakthrough album *Born to Run* had just come out. With Devin and Joani, we shared your basic Jewish stuff, along with sports. Joani was an excellent tennis player, and Devin a softball player and excellent athlete, who I nevertheless beat more often than not in ping pong. Lastly, Tom and Nore were on their way to grad school in psychology, and each had a shared interest in the exploration of bodywork: yoga, meditation, and bioenergetic therapy, a body-oriented form of therapy which stressed releasing emotional energy blocks lodged in the body. Every one of the counselors there was interesting to me, and likeable, and I felt genuinely liked by them in return. Of course, my relationship with Will was the deepest. We were doing twice-a-week therapy, and he was on to my bullshit, and increasingly called me on it in a nice way, while making me feel like I was ok just as I was. Not anything I had ever experienced from a therapist before and I was strongly feeling the positive effects of the relationship. So, in mid-November, my dad informed me that he would be coming to San Francisco to make a visit, and he wanted to meet me and my therapist Will.

Dad had finally re-married following a blistering flurry of dating. About nine months before his visit to me in the Bay, he met a medical social worker named Olga, who was my mother's age, attractive, and seemingly nice. I had not met her yet, but Dad was happy with the choice he had made, and I was happy for him that he wouldn't be alone anymore. Dad still worked full time in his cardiology practice in Manhattan, and still did his watercolor painting in his spare time, a hobby he had picked up while in the army in Italy in World War II. He seemed pretty good at it, I thought. He knew something about perspective, which is about as much as I knew about painting, not having painted very much, except the one or two times I had made some watercolors and pastels with Dad on vacations when I was younger. Dad seemed to have a knack for it, and had had instruction. I was too impatient and not very visual, so I was not very good at it. I was drawn more to the performing arts like acting and singing, where I was told I had some talent, but of course had not had the focus or discipline, or maybe the desire to pursue acting more seriously.

Dad came to visit on a Thursday in mid-November, and was glad to see me, but I could tell he had a look of cautious optimism about him. He had been through a lot, dealing with my shit over the years, and had grown skeptical, if not downright pessimistic, that I would ever stabilize or get my shit together, as my generation liked to say. This was something I sensed. I'm sure he would never say it to my face. But there was a quality of tired resignation about him. Until he met Will.

Will was very upbeat about me during our three-way meeting. He framed my problem as a delayed adolescence and identity conflict that he felt confident I was working through. Dad, in his clinical investigator form of relating, asked Will a lot of tough questions, about whether I could work, whether I could ever sustain a relationship. It was hard to hear, but in Will, I felt I had not just a champion, but someone who sincerely believed I was on the right road. It made me feel more confident. After our meeting, Dad was beside himself with relief. He really liked Will, and felt like I was in good hands, and in his demeanor, I sensed that he too felt I might get my shit together and have a life. Things were starting to go in a good direction. But I could still be spacey, and moody, and easily set off, with a lot of anger. I really didn't know if I had what it took to tolerate the stresses and strains of a job. But apparently some people did. About two weeks after Dad's visit to Phoenix, Tim sat me down for our usual one to-one.

Tim said, "There's something I have to tell you. On January 1, I'm leaving. I've been offered a new job in Monterey, to help start a new halfway house, the first of its kind in Monterey County. I'll be in from the ground floor. I'll be working with Barry Nelles, the guy who had Will's job before Will, who I like, who is a really smart guy. That's the bad news. The good news is, Barry is a very progressive, out-there thinker, and he asked me to see if I could come up with a resident, someone who has gone through the experience of being a mental patient, and lived in a halfway house, to be part of the counseling staff. And I came up with you. I think you'd be great. You're smart, you can relate. You were the first person that came to mind. What do you think?"

I was both scared and excited. "Wow," I said, "I don't know what to think. I think I would love it. I can't believe that you guys would be willing to take that chance, but yes I'd like to try."

"I know you counseled a little before your girlfriend was killed, so you'll be good, but you should think about it for a bit and get back to me. I spoke to Will, and he wants you to get your feet wet by doing some night watchman duties first, to see how that goes, to see how comfortable you would be."

Still flabbergasted, I said, "Yeah, I think that would be good. Wow, I'm still dazed by this. I kind of always thought I could be good at this, but never thought I would get another chance. Wow. I just don't know what to say."

I began doing night watchman duties every Saturday night for the next month, and into the new year. I looked forward to doing it, but I had some worries about how my fellow residents might feel. I was worried that they might resent me, given my new special status, worried that they might perceive me as arrogant or superior, particularly because I felt I had a special connection with the other staff members. I felt caught in the middle. Maybe I was more articulate, better read, more with it. Something. There was a difference, but I tried not to be arrogant about it. There were a couple of residents who took potshots at me as I assumed my night watch duties, but I handled it. Most residents were cool, and some even glad that one of their own was moving up. Luckiest of all, the place was quiet during my shift. Three or four residents stayed up with me until 2am watching TV, the usual nightwatch activity when no one was in crisis, which was getting increasingly common. The problems at the house were more connected to depression, social isolation, and withdrawal, requiring less immediate response, so at night, people were left alone. They knew where to find me - on the couch in the main house - if they needed to talk, which never happened. Things went smoothly into the new year.

CHAPTER 24

Jung in January (1976)

The first few days of January were unusually cold, rainy and overcast. Dank. I should have been feeling on top of the world, having been offered a new job, deemed competent and stable enough to do nightwatch work, and had even been given a stamp of confidence by my father, not to mention the ongoing support and encouragement of Will and the staff, yet a feeling of doom and deep gloom overtook me. I couldn't sleep. And it wasn't because I was overstimulated. No, I was in an anxiety state, the likes of which I hadn't felt since my first hospitalization at age eighteen at the Institute of Living, when I freaked out after the singing of *"We Gotta Get Out of This Place,"* and experienced a two week nightly panic state from which I needed shots of Thorazine to calm down. This time it felt like it came out of nowhere. I vowed not to take any medications.

Todd, a young man of the gay persuasion, who had been a patient at Phoenix a few years previously, was on nightwatch duty during the first few nights of this. Clearly, this guy was in touch with his vulnerable side, after he'd been through the stresses of stigma as a gay child and teen, growing up in a conservative California town. Todd had experienced severe depression, even trying to kill himself years earlier, but now he had a comfort with who he was, and his own vulnerability seemed to be his strength. Todd could see I was in distress. It was pretty obvious to the naked eye. I had a worried and scared look on my face. Todd gave me a mantra. Part of it was about encouraging me to breathe as a way of calming myself, which in the throes of an anxiety state was minimally helpful. Breathing was a good thing to do as a way to calm down. But when you were in the midst of deep anxiety or panic, well that just wasn't gonna do anything at all. One of the things I was doing was fighting the feeling. The anxiety. The more I tried to push it away, the worse it got. It was so uncomfortable that at its worst I thought I was going to die. No distinctions between the physical and psychological. Todd was staying very close by. And he said one big thing to me that I took to heart. It changed my life. Todd said, "Rather than fight your anxiety, welcome your anxiety. Your anxiety, after all, is a part of you, and when you're fighting it, you're fighting a part of yourself. What you have to try and do is say to the anxiety, 'It's okay to feel anxious, it's ok to be anxious.' The more you can let yourself flow with the feeling, the sooner it will go away. So in other words, don't fight the fear, it will just make it worse."

Easier said than done, but Todd was not wrong. By Todd's third nightshift, I was able to begin to shift my perspective. I started to internalize Todd's message, and tell myself that being anxious was ok, and that the more I was ok with the feeling, the sooner it would pass. I swear to God it worked, because once I began to go with the flow, the sooner my anxiety began to dissipate. I was giving the anxiety nothing to hit up against. I was no longer fighting myself, or my feelings, or more specifically, my anxiety. And by the end of the week I was back. But not before I had put myself through hell, what Carl Jung called the "dark night of the soul." When my anxiety became much more manageable, I was able to think for the first time with clarity about what might have been going on with me. The thing that stood out was I was afraid of success. Failure was like an identity, and the idea that I could be a regular, functional, maybe even eventually somewhat happy member of society, even though it was something I really wanted, made me feel scared to death. A Bob Dylan line kept reverberating in my head after I came down from the anxiety and panic attacks. It was a line from his song "Love Minus Zero/No Limit" from his *Bringing it All Back Home* album. "There's no success like failure, and failure's no success at all." Dylan described my dilemma to a tee, and my identity on the deepest level. With my anxiety gone, I could think again, and the Dylan line made the most sense regarding the origin of my fears. Todd's strategy saved me. I had lucked out, finding the right person at the right time with the right solution. But I must confess that I still wasn't completely out of the woods. During and after that week, I worried about what Will and Tim would think about me, and whether it really was a good idea for me to move to Monterey in June. Whether I was together enough. If Tim and Will were concerned, they did not let on. They continued to convey their confidence in me, and attempted to contextualize what I'd been going through. Fear of growing up, fear of being an adult, fear of being a failure, fear of proving my dad wrong. All these things had been with me a long time, and were hard to shake. But their faith in me was steadfast. But I won't lie to you; even though I had learned a valuable lesson about panic and anxiety from Todd, and even though I had gained some understanding about what my anxiety was saying, and even with the show of confidence from Will and Tim, that week in panic land made me question whether I would be ready to work with my fellow crazies in a position of responsibility. I took a week off from my nightwatchman weekend duties to allow myself to regroup. The week had taken it out of me. I slept a lot, and was more socially withdrawn than I had been before .The only thing I wanted to do was listen to Dylan's recent record, "Blood on the Tracks," or read some of my friend Ricky's object relations books he had given me from his time in the Bay Area. I read up on Harry Guntrip and his idea of the regressed ego, the most primitive mental layer, and his way of describing the psyche made sense of what I had been going through. The week to retool was helpful, but I was not yet 100%. My so-called dark night of the soul had left me gun shy, and I was quite reserved around residents and staff. Still depressed, my confidence was shaken. And I would stay that way for quite a while.

CHAPTER 25

Almost Independent (January-March 1976)

Back to myself minus some self-confidence, I felt as though I were back in a hole. Maybe I needed that, I told myself, because I felt even though I was depressed, I now had a more realistic view of what I was facing. I was scared, yes, but maybe that was realistic. Moving to a strange town would be a leap. Starting a new job, maybe a new career, would be a leap too, but maybe something that through my own travails, I was now qualified for. The bravado was gone. The Bogart persona was suddenly not there to protect me. My Montgomery Clift, sensitive, vulnerable, hurt, compassionate side moved to the forefront. The days and nights at Phoenix, while once a fascination, and even fun, now became a kind of dull drudgery. The daily routine of waking up, going to the day center, attending the groups, and talking to the same residents and staff and day center clients, was deadening. I was depressed, but very in touch with reality, or so I told myself. Just before Christmas, I advanced from the Far Out House to the Green House, the last stage. I was on my way out. Tim was gone, off to Monterey to help Barry Nelles start a new social rehab program named Interim. I had a new female counselor named Anne, and soon she became involved with Will, my therapist, who had been married twice, and was now a widower. Anne was a plainspoken, kind, practical, down-to-earth person. She and I had a bond, but not the tight bond I had felt with Tim. In some ways, guys were easier to talk to than girls, as I felt I could let loose some of my more inappropriate thoughts and feelings more easily. The feminism of the day, however, was very much about equality, and the breakdown of differences between males and females, so to talk as if there were differences was not popular or desirable. Even though Anne struck me as a sturdy sort, I just didn't feel right discussing my salacious thoughts or vicious fantasies with her. Luckily, I still had Will for that. But as I was in what felt like my more Montgomery Clift sensitive phase, feeling depressed, reserved, and somewhat passive, it didn't matter much. I had to feel comfortable and confident to let those thoughts fly. When I was depressed, my inhibitions came back.

My conversations with Anne were frequently about the transition I would soon be making out of Phoenix House and into independent living. In a month or so, in mid-March, I would be moving into satellite housing in the community. I guess I was feeling ready, although in my now depressed state, I wasn't getting a kick out of anything, rather, just going through the motions. The only new wrinkle that was at all interesting was a burgeoning relationship with a new counselor by the name of Betty. She was a bright, feisty blonde, single and unattached, who took a liking to me. I should say more than a liking; an attraction that was mutual. I liked her. She was easy to talk to, and one night, about a month before my transition to satellite housing, we were in my room at the Green House talking about I don't know what, when the next thing I knew, we were making out. Now, of course this was against the rules, but rules, schmules. It was hot and forbidden. As Betty was a new counselor, trying to do well and gain respect, she immediately saw the error of her ways. And being an honest or guilty sort, hard to know which, she felt duty bound to report this to Will, her supervisor. Will was not pleased, but in his non-judgmental way, he told Betty to knock it off. Without trying to make her feel too bad about herself, he calmly but clearly stated that fraternizing between staff and residents was inappropriate, and too confusing for all parties. There had to be some boundaries, even though the program was trying to create a family feeling in the community. An incestuous family was probably not a healthy model. Will communicated this to Betty without shaming her, while still getting his point across. This was her rationale for why we needed to cease and desist all sexual contact. I was not surprised in the least, but I must admit the whole thing was kind of a rush. After all, I got off on being an object of staff affection, which gave me the jolt of self-esteem that I needed at that point, but unfortunately not enough to get me out of my depression. I still had to leave Phoenix House, and face moving to Monterey. A little dalliance was only a momentary palliative. My life was feeling daunting. Could I do it? I was looking the facts square in the face, determined to try, but not knowing what the outcome would be.

CHAPTER 26

Satellite Housing (March-June 1976)

I moved out of Phoenix on St. Patrick's Day, 1976. Not that I celebrated by going to an Irish bar. I wasn't drinking much. I wasn't doing much. I moved in with four other people, a mile down the road, into a 1950s non-descript ranch-style house that Phoenix had purchased for residents wanting to get their feet wet in independent living. My batch of roommates would be the first in this new experiment of living in the community. All of my new roommates, including three who had been old roommates at the Green House, were veterans of nut houses. Suicide attempts, schizophrenic breakdowns, that kind of thing. Most of them, including myself, were on minimal to no meds. None of us had jobs. All of us were on permanent disability (SSI). All of us were in our mid to late 20s. There was a couple, Sarah and Joe, who had hooked up while residents at Phoenix. Loretta was a strawberry blonde, who had been quite attractive when she first arrived at Phoenix, but had put on fifty pounds and seemed to have lost her confidence about her sex appeal with males. Finally, there was Regina, a beautiful, petite, light-brown-haired woman about my age, who unfortunately, seemed kind of frozen. She talked about trivialities. Not too bright. We started out as roommates. We should have stayed that way. She looked like a Barbie Doll, and her superficial way of talking had me confused. I couldn't tell if it was the result of the traumas she had been through, or that she suffered from NVS syndrome (not very smart). Either way, she was fun to look at, but not a lot else. We mostly passed the time watching TV. My reading capacity during this period waxed and waned. Mostly waned. Often the three of us would sit in the sparsely decorated living room watching game shows or sit-coms, which was pretty boring, but given my depressed, withdrawn state, was about as much as I could handle.

One night in mid-April, a month after moving into the new satellite situation, Loretta and Regina had too much wine. Loretta excused herself after a while, leaving Regina and me in the living room together. Sloppily, Regina made an advance, saying that she had found me attractive for a while, and that we could go into her bedroom if I liked. I liked, even though I had been told by my father, you don't shit where you eat, or some such aphorism. I thought of it as the separation of church and state. It could get messy. But the dick wants what it wants, and I didn't say no. It was bad sex. Regina, despite the fact that she was tipsy, was very stiff. It was almost like having sex with a mechanical doll. Regina didn't know how to loosen up. She was going through the motions. Her body was saying no, her mind saying yes. Clearly her mind and body were not on speaking terms. It wasn't fun. And we both vowed the next day to remain friends, because it just wasn't worth it. I escaped any significant ramifications or consequences of the rather risky deed I participated in, because lucky for me, Regina was so cut off, or oblivious, or stupid, that she was able to act as though nothing had happened from there on in. This was fine with me, as I didn't need the complications or unnecessary tension. In retrospect, that event was the house highlight. I too was kind of cut off from myself, and from others. But despite this, I was determined to try to reclaim some of the pieces of my past life before having been a resident of Phoenix, as part of my strategy for returning to normal and getting ready for Monterey. I enrolled again in classes at Jean Shelton, where I took another scene study class with Jean. I resumed playing softball on weekends in Berkeley with my old cohorts. In both places, I felt like a literal shadow of my former self. As stiff as Regina had been in bed, I was almost as stiff in the acting school, rehearsing my scene. In my ridiculous grandiosity, I took on the part of Jamie in *Long Day's Journey into Night*, by O'Neill. A huge task for a seasoned actor, it was a joke for a fledgling one. In my withdrawn state, I couldn't get outside of myself, or get loose enough to get into the role. It was painful, and I lasted six weeks before I gave up for good, both the class and any idea of becoming an actor. I didn't have the chops. The decision was a relief. Fuck it, I thought, maybe I could do some good in the mental health world. That would remain to be seen.

Softball was another story. I didn't have to interact that much, could escape into the game, and my mates mostly left me alone to just play, which also was a relief. I was very self- conscious, but doing my best, and determined to begin to live some semblance of a normal life, which the acting class was supposed to represent and the softball actually did represent. I also started up my night watchman duties at the house again. All of these activities were part of my normalization preparation for re-entry back into mainstream society. I could feel my fear, but I could also feel my determination. Six weeks to go before Monterey.

In the middle of May, Phoenix Program hosted a camping trip to Yosemite. Including staff and residents from the house, and staff and clients from the center, when we arrived on a Tuesday, the campsites were not very crowded. It was two weeks before the official start of the camping and visiting season at Yosemite. The counselors had booked a campsite near Tuolumne Meadows, in a beautiful area, surrounded by big trees and a nearby waterfall. In a rerun of my experience as a resident at Phoenix, I felt much more of a connection to the staff of Phoenix than I did any of the residents or center clients. Yet I wasn't a staff member. I was in some kind of no man's land. Staff were their usual kind, compassionate, regular selves, yet facts were facts. I wasn't staff. Residents and center clients just did not seem to be in the same place as me. Less intellectual, I don't know what it was.

I found myself obsessing about my new job, the potential that a new life held, and took some consolation in the beauty of the place when I could allow myself to take it in. The waterfalls, the trees, the mountains, the wildlife were a lot to take in, and when my mind was freed up, the natural beauty of Tuolumne was serene. Unfortunately, my self-absorption dominated, so my experience of its beauty was minimal. My worry or anticipation about my future life in Monterey vacillated between fear and occasionally excitement. About eight parts worry and fear, and about two parts excitement and looking forward. On the good side, I thought I knew enough about counseling and therapy after all this time. I had accumulated six years of therapy and three long hospitalizations, if you counted my stay at Phoenix. One could say, when looking at it from that angle, that I had a lot of experience. What I lacked was a kind of confidence that only comes from actual counseling experience, plus the belief that I could handle any stress or strain that might come from dealing with actively disturbed people. My track record in dealing with the bumps and bruises of my own life had not been very good up to this point. I hadn't handled my three major relationships very well. Two breakups had led to severe reactions, resulting in hospitalizations. One relationship had resulted in a hospitalization in the beginning phase, maybe as a result of a desire to have an open relationship. Whatever the cause, I hadn't handled these significant attachments very well, assuming, of course, that my troubles were a result of environmental stress or psychological causes. Then again, my problems could be biological. After all this time, it was still up in the air, but the bottom line was, I had to learn how to cope with stress and responsibilities, whatever the cause of my mental health problems.

CHAPTER 27

The Facts on the Ground (June-July 1976)

A month before lift off. The mundane structure of my life remained the same. The only difference was that I met with Will, my therapist, two times a week, but now at his home in Berkeley, where I also babysat his six- year old son. Will continued to pump me up with encouragement, while at the same time, making room for me to express my fears, worries and reservations. Moving away from the Bay Area, where I had made my home, would be a big change. Even though I hadn't lived in Berkeley for a year now, I still had friends there, even if I hadn't seen them very much in the past year. I contacted Doug, and Statman, and Hal, and saw them each a couple of times, informing them of my situation and plan to move to Monterey. They were all positive, part of my "return to normal" project. Devin, one of the Phoenix counselors, even invited me to his house for a birthday barbecue with his girlfriend Ellen and some of his friends, which felt to me like a kind of coming out party for arriving back into the world of the normal.

Devin had always treated me like a peer, maybe because that's the way we had initially known each other, as rival softball players and fellow partygoers. Whatever it was, he was nonchalant about my being at his barbecue, which helped in casting off my resident status, and returning to some equal ground with the people I respected. I got a burst of self-confidence from that small gesture. However, I was still depressed, and dealing with the residue from my week back in January, which I now referred to as my dark night of the soul, a la Jung. But I was acting as if I was normal, despite how I felt. The whole month of June was devoted to getting my acting chops together. If I couldn't perform on the stage, then I was going to use acting to function in my life. Fake it till you make it was how the saying goes. And that's what I was going to do. In looking back at my first hospitalization back in Hartford in 1968, I realized then that that was what I had to do to convince the shrinks I could leave the hospital. It was an act. But a necessary act. You had to show people that you could act normal. People mostly weren't interested in how you felt. Maybe, if you were lucky, there were two or three people who were interested. The rest could give a shit. So that would be the deal. It's what everybody else did. My sense after all this time was that everybody was fucked up. You had to learn how to hide your feelings. My mistake in my breakdowns was believing that the truth would set me free. I was wrong. My grandmother, who I had never met, had actually had it right when she said, "The truth is not wanted."

When it came to functioning in this world, nobody wanted the truth, most people wanted to be bullshitted, and that was enough. But I had learned that the people who loved you, and the people you loved, could handle honesty and full expression of feeling. The rest could give a shit. From here on in, the mask would be on. As an old racetrack buddy had once asked, "Am I ready for the public?" I now knew what he meant. Gotta put on that mask, keep it on until it's safe. Be a pretender. Then, when it was safe with loved ones, you could be yourself again. It was as simple as that. That was the mantra. As I began to pack up what little stuff I had in preparation for moving to Monterey, I realized that I had a new task: figuring out when it was safe to be myself, and with whom, and when it was not. The other thing that occurred to me was that I had to learn, maybe for the first time, not to take things so personally. Have a harder shell. Grow a pair. All those expressions for learning how to cope with the "slings and arrows of outrageous fortune," or the world, or life, or people. All of it, and some of it. I had to be ready. I vowed to myself that this time I would listen to the old Dylan admonition. "Time will tell who has fell and who's been left behind." Time to man up. I was twenty-six years old. Perhaps a little late in the game. But I had arrived: good times, bad times, good mood, bad mood, happy, sad. It was time to be an adult. I was ready. Time to play the game. Scared but determined. Mask on, sometimes firmly, sometimes loosely, sometimes hopefully, or no mask at all. Five hospitalizations and recoveries. Now, heading down highway 17 south to Monterey alone, my sixth beginning. Scared. Would I, could I make it work? I didn't know. I couldn't know. I was determined to try. And then, around Santa Cruz, a surge of adrenalized self-confidence. Fucking A, I could, fucking A, I would. Onward and upward, motherfuckers! But really, in truth, there was no way to know what was ahead. Just the unknown, and me, and the rest of my life. A lot of maybes. Maybe, maybe, maybe. "Maybe baby." Okay Buddy Holly! Maybe. The Chantels. Still crazy, did it matter? Mind loose, mind tight. Watsonville, Castroville, artichokes, Marina, Seaside, Fort Ord, the acrid smell of seaweed, swirling wind off the cypress trees, Monterey. I'm here. I'm home.

WHAT IF PART ONE

(JULY 22, 1971–MAY 1, 1973)

Mandatory 8 Count 2 Harding Hospital (July 22, 1971)

Fucking out of it. I have my brother Dave, my sister-in-law Cherise, and my girlfriend Carole in tow when I arrive at another nuthouse. I am going nowhere fast. Three years out of high school, two years of college completed, four hospitalizations. I am fucked. I am disheartened and angry. Frustrated. Here comes the fucking straight jacketing meds. Haldol and Cogentin. Diagnosis: paranoid schizophrenia. Wrong. It will be another thirteen years before that is straightened out. Whatever. This is now, and this sucks.

So now I'm back in. Maybe the nuthouse is where I belong. Fuckin' loser. I'm pissed at myself, pissed at the world. Ah, now I get it. This is the place for "mad men." I definitely qualify for that. I see a couple of hippies, as pissed as me in their own ways. One guy, Tom, keeps shaking his head in disbelief, like, *what the fuck happened?* He tells me he had the world on a string, dealing dope, getting stoned all day every day, tripping, fucking a lot of women, living in fucking Jamaica, and what happens, he can't fucking stand it, so he goes fucking crazy. This other guy, Scott , he's a real nut job. He barely talks, he just davens, rocking back and forth, with his long black hair blowing in the wind. When he does talk, he's like some weird genius. He tells me I'm in "reactive mind" or something. What the fuck is that? Then he starts to explain to me about Dianetics. You know, Scientology. And how it's the real truth about how the mind works. And it's pretty compelling stuff, except the shrinks here think he's a fucking lunatic. It's hard to know who's right. He does a lot of yelling about how fucking nuts the shrinks are. They keep medicating the shit out of him. Social control at work.

I don't know what to think. They're all fucking nuts if you ask me. I like this guy Tom better. He's more my cup of tea. At least you can have a conversation with the guy that isn't clichés, and incoherent psychospeak. He at least has ONE foot on the ground. At least the ground I'm familiar with. He just seems too stoned and spacey. Not nuts. Not psychotic. Me, I'm prone to free association rants, a la Dylan's "Subterranean Homesick Blues." My mind just seems to fly off the handle; it's fun, interesting. People have no idea what the fuck I'm talking about half the time. It's like I'm in my own little world. They don't get the references, but the references make sense to me. They come from rock songs, movies, occasionally from books, and occasionally from people I know who said funny shit. Whatever, it doesn't matter. I'm stuck inside of the nut house. "Stuck inside of Mobile with the Memphis Blues Again." I'm in prison, except once again I didn't resist, I went of my own volition. As if I had no other choice. Carole was opposed, and I allowed her to be overruled, spineless prick that I am. Now what? I am going to be here awhile. I know this drill. Stabilize me on meds, get me used to the hospital routine (structure), earn privileges, gain access to the outside world, then after I have been sufficiently institutionalized, and develop fears and phobias regarding the outside world, learn how to deal with my fear and lowered self-esteem. Then I'll feel more comfortable in the nuthouse. Less motivated to be out of the nuthouse. Then, I'll slowly get used to being out again, while straightjacketed on the fucking meds. I am gonna do six months of this bullshit. That's right. Carole will come to visit me once a week, every week, for months. She will call me two or three times a week. She's very faithful, loyal, loving, and understanding. Angry with these fucking people as well. Probably angry with me too, but she doesn't express it. Mostly, we are united in our anti- establishment, anti-psychiatry view of the nuthouse, victimized by it, but too scared, and I'm ultimately too numbed out to bolt from it.

This time it will take me about six weeks until zombiehood arrives, the state in which passivity, and mental paralysis appears, and one becomes listless and compliant to the requests of the powers that be. Haldol having done its thing, I will sleep a lot, listen to music, follow the rules, and be a good little boy with minimal resistance or will. My dick doesn't work either. I can't ejaculate. Lovely. Carole is dutiful and loving. I have lucked out in my life. Two long hospitalizations, two caring loving women. Marla and Carole. It's nice that they see something in me that I cannot see currently. I am a shadow of my former self that wasn't that hot to begin with. When Carole came that first day with my brother, she was so sad and so loving. She took me in her arms and we both just sobbed for ten minutes. And then when Dave and Cherise left, because they needed to get to the airport to fly back to Madison, it was just Carole and me on the Harding grounds, so defeated, but Carole buoyed me up. We made plans for my leaving soon, and then moving into an apartment that we would be getting together. Carole was so hopeful, determined and loving. "These fucking shrinks don't know shit," she said. "They know nothing about feelings, Arnie. All they know is to shut people down, suppress them, numb them. Social control motherfuckers. I'm gonna spring you out. Give me a week to hatch a plan. Ok Arnie?"

I tried to listen, but I was in and out, loose associating in an angry way, nodding, but all the while pacing and chain smoking my Viceroys.

I am in full agreement with Carole, but not fully there. I go in and out of rants, and have a hard time staying focused on a conversation. I'm loose associating like a motherfucker, but I say as much as I can that I'm in with the scheme. Carole says it will take her two weeks to hatch the plan, and then we will be home free. It's late July. The plan for my escape will be set for Saturday August 6 at noon. We will talk by phone daily after my initial meeting with her at Harding. And then she will come visit every Saturday for the next two weeks just to make sure I still want to do it, and to fill me in on the details of the "liberation." But each week she comes, I become weaker, the meds starting to take hold. I'm tired a lot, and my feelings starting to numb. I'm less angry, less hyper, and by the time August 6 comes around, despite Carole's work to spring me from the looney bin, despite her desire, despite my desire, despite our ideological opposition to the ways and means of the fucking medical model bullshit running of the hospital, despite all that. Why do I comply and take my meds instead of cheeking them? Why don't I just fucking rebel? Why? Because I 'm weak. And Carole won't go through with springing me unless I'm in all the way. Being batshit crazy is one thing. Carole thinks she can handle that. But the resigned, submissive me, giving in to the doctors, the meds, is another thing entirely. The plan won't work that way. She needs me to be strong, active, and angry. Willing. What the fuck is wrong with me? I want Carole more than anyone I've ever wanted. She wants me. In fact, she is ready to fight for me. Risk getting into trouble for me. But me. Why do I decide to take the meds? Why go along with a system I hate? Maybe it was because I'm in agony. Being manic, being crazy is very tiring and intense. You're always getting weird looks from people but you're too speeded up to pay them any mind. As awful as the meds are, and they are awful, they bring a kind of relief from the relentless, hyper-energetic, disinhibited way of being. If I don't take the meds, I could be high for days, months, and won't get anything done. I'd already been through that two summers before. It all stinks. My sweet Carole, I can't and won't put her through that. It's just that the alternative is just as bad, maybe worse. So I wuss out. Ashamed, with my head between my legs, by August 6, the alleged date of the springing, I am in no shape. I am a shadow of the man I had been and Carole knows it. It is obvious. She is extremely disappointed, sad, a little mad at me but mostly at the hospital establishment, the doctors, Dr. Leuchter. Ah, but I don't know what else to do. I go the zombie route. Comply with doctor's orders and lose the next five months of my life. Then I lose my girl in seven.

During the time at Harding, dutiful Carole still visited me every week. Every Saturday on the dot. She bolstered my morale, held me, encouraged me. So by December, five months later, I earned a visit to her pad back on the OSU campus. I stayed over for the weekend and had crappy sex for the first time in five months. The meds made erections tough, made orgasms tough, made feeling my feelings tough, made feeling my sensations tough. But it was still better than nothing. A week later I would be released when Dr. Leuchter found a hospital housekeeper, a Seventh Day Adventist , to put me up in her house, and whip a little religion into me as I began employment at a restaurant in Worthington, the town where Harding hospital was. Once again working as a dishwasher, I was depressed, with low energy. Quiet and pacified. Dead. Two months of this. Misery central. Carole was still a constant presence, but in January she found out she was pregnant, and went to New York, where abortion was legal, before Roe v. Wade, and got the procedure. Of course, in my misery, depression, and low functioning, I didn't have it together enough to go with her to New York. Regret City.

A month later, Leuchter waved the white flag. Gave up. He told me, "I've done what I can. It's time for you to go back to New York and live with your dad. It ain't working out here."

Even Carole, although super sad and distraught, couldn't disagree. I was a mess. Pretty unavailable to her. Depressed. Too quiet. She had her life to live. Classes to go to. A bachelor's degree to get. Maybe the move to New York would be for the best. She swore to stay in touch weekly, as she had done during my hospitalization. I believed her. And she came through. But now it was time to return to the Rotten Apple.

That was the thumbnail sketch of what happened from July 1971 to February 1972. Here are some more details of what happened during those seven months. Summer became fall. George Jackson was killed. Attica happened. American Pie was number one on the Top 40 list. The war raged on. In October, Leuchter set it up for me to get me a job in the hospital cafeteria. I started working as a dishwasher in the hospital kitchen, and did a good enough job. Then my shrink, sensing I was both stable and functional enough, tried to enlist the help of the hospital social worker to find me work in the outside world, and succeeded at a nearby restaurant, once again as a dishwasher. It was now five months into my stay at Harding. Time to move out, but Dr. Leuchter decided that my best move was to stay close to the hospital and near my new job as a dishwasher. Carole was upset, but understanding. She told me that Dr. Leuchter had encouraged her to not get her hopes up about me. She said he had told her, more or less, that I was a lost cause, that people like me didn't get better, and she'd be better off finding someone else. Hearing this hurt and enraged me. But I was too weakened to do much about it in the short run. It became a battle cry later on, unbeknownst to me at the time. It lit a flame inside of me that would serve me for the rest of my life.

Then, however, I took up residence with one of the cleaning women at Harding, who rented me a room in her house. She was a devout Seventh Day Adventist, the church that underwrote the not so lovely Harding Hospital. Those people didn't eat meat, drink or go to church on Sunday. Sabbath on Saturday, like we Jews. Fundamentalistisch. They're big on soy foods. Basically vegetarian. Of course, she tried to whip a little Jesus on me, which, for this little Jew boy, only furthered my alienation, isolation, and ever deepening depression. To be honest, this Jesus stuff coming from these earnest forthright Christians gave me the willies, always has. I worked at the restaurant. I hated it. Once again, I had less and less to say to people, just like a year ago in Madison, after another depression. I was despondent and defeated, and even Carole's visits to me were not lifting me up. Even though we finally had sex for the first time in five months, it was not the same. I was too down. Not myself.

By February of 1972, Dr Leuchter and my father discussed my situation over the phone, and we agreed that going back to New Rochelle seemed the only plausible move. Carole informed me a week later that she was pregnant from our December escapade. We agreed she needs an abortion. Abortion was illegal in Ohio but legal in New York. My father, good doctor and good liberal that he was, intervened and arranged it in one of the hospital clinics he knew in Manhattan. Carole came to New York and got the procedure done. It was sad and sadder that I couldn't be there for her, emotionally or physically. There, in New York, my father, maybe influenced by Leuchter, maybe from having come to this determination on his own, told Carole that she should move on from me. That I was not going to get better, and that more than likely, if she stuck with me, she was gonna be dealing with a sick man for the rest of her life. In similar words, but in a separate conversation, my brother Lew confided in me that Dad said the same thing to him as well. But Lew didn't tell me this for a while, only after Carole did. It only added to my fucked-upness.

The foray in Ohio lasted three years. I left Carole in Columbus and moved back to New Rochelle, depressed and defeated, but not permanently.

CHAPTER 2

Torn and Tattered New York (February 1972 – May 1973)

New York was not how I pictured it, a la Stevie Wonder's song, "Living in the City." It was bleak, gray, and cold, and those were its good qualities. Back in New Rochelle, I was a two-time college dropout, without my woman. What was I doing here? Confused, but without the will or strength to direct my life, I was back with my dad and my brother Lew, who was now a senior in high school. We agreed I would start seeing a shrink, and find something to do. Perhaps some kind of training, so I could earn a living. Dr. Makeover, the new shrink, knew of a vocational program in the Bronx, called Altro, where they trained disabled people to do various trades, including garment trades, and printing trades. I agreed to participate, as the academic track was going nowhere, my concentration shot, and my motivation and goal setting minimal. Time to change course.

Change course I did. Starting in April of 1972, after a six week hiatus of doing nothing other than shrinking and odd jobs around the house, I began my on-the-job-training at Altro, an apprenticeship in photo offset printing in the South Bronx, the Hunts Point stop on the number 2 line of the IRT from 241st in Mount Vernon. My Dad drove me initially until I figured out the bus lines. At Altro, run by the American Jewish Federation, and populated by mentally and developmentally disabled young adults, I met a variety of folks. Irish, Italian, Black, and Puerto Rican, plus a smattering of Jews. My supervisor, Milt Goldstein, was a Jewish Leftist, a veteran of the Abraham Lincoln Brigade, and a former Trotskyist. Goldstein was a great guy, funny, and sort of no nonsense. He left the teaching to the more senior apprentices at the print shop, who I partnered up with. In the shop, I learned how to do stripping, plate making, and the actual photo offset printing on a 1500 multilith printer. One color. Black and white press. I was adequate in this job, but inferior to many other co- apprentices, who possessed what I believed were inferior IQ's, yet who were three times as fast as me on the press, and just as accurate. In printing, speed and accuracy are at a premium. This is true in particular in small commercial shops where the profit margin is so slight. So, at Altro they were sticklers for teaching you first accuracy, and then speed combined with accuracy. This was also the proper procedure for learning how to be an effective pitcher. First control, and then velocity.

This training gig lasted nine months. I was paid at minimum wage. But I lived at home rent free. For the first six months I did very little socializing, other than with Lew and Dad. Occasionally, I went out with Dad and his current girlfriend Lily Tansenberg, a hot, but somewhat phony woman, clearly gold-digging. My dad liked the sex. At least that's what he told me. My dad's boundaries were a little porous. He filled me in on the unsolicited details of his sex life after my mom's death, and also filled me in on the details of his sex life with my mom, which I really didn't want to hear about. But my protests went unheeded. It must also be said that I must have been a little curious, because I never left the room when he went into his sexual reveries or conquest tales, despite my squeamishness and protestations to the contrary. Incestuous voyeurism, vicarious primal scene stuff at work here I guess. Some fucked up shit.

From February to July, I had no social contact with any women, until I went to Ohio to spend my vacation with Carole, who had maintained phone contact with me back in New York, despite Leuchter's admonitions to the contrary. It didn't go well. There was a sense of distance between us. It felt like Carole had moved on psychologically on some level. I think we slept together once, and it was not that good. By the end of the two weeks in the middle of July, upon returning to New Rochelle, I resolved to get back into the dating, womanizing game.

Feeling sad about Carole, and slightly pissed, but sort of understanding where she was coming from, I started hitting the Park View Bar again, in south New Rochelle, near the Long Island Sound. The Park View at this time was the reigning bar in New Rochelle for the college and post-college crowd. They had big crowds even during the week. I did well, scoring-wise. Between August and May of the next year, I picked up four women, two for one-nighters. One alone, and the other with my friend Rick and another girl he fancied. The other two lasted a bit longer. Maybe a month or so. One, Robyn, turned me on to my first hit of coke ever. We got together a few times until it ended up in Boston on a bad weekend, where she was attending school, when her crabbiness in general, and particularly towards me, turned me off completely, both interpersonally and sexually. Cathy Komen was another case completely. She was a little sweetie. Eighteen, and a senior in high school, who, as it turned out, I had met from Shenorock, the summer place owned by my relatives on my mother's side. My aunts - Mary, Janis, and Florie, my mother's sisters - were friends with the Komens. Cathy had a brother, an ADHD type kid, a wild man who everyone called Dynamite. Anyway, the night I met Cathy at the Park View, she was wearing this cool white sheepskin coat from Israel, or so she told me as I complimented her on her jacket, which quickly led to us making a date for New Year's Eve on the Island. We got it on on our first date, and got together several times after for about six weeks until it became clear that we had nothing in common. The age and intellect gaps were too great.

By January of 1973, my printing skills were sufficiently developed that Milt, the supervisor, agreed to start putting out feelers for jobs. I soon got one at Hudson Press in the printing district in lower Manhattan. But it was not a good fit. They had me on a three letter Davidson press, which I was not used to, and the pace was too frenetic and pressured for my level of competence. I lasted three days before I was history. But a day or two later, another gig came up with United Feature Syndicate in the Daily News building on 42nd street and Lexington Ave in Manhattan, close to Grand Central station. It was a full-time mailroom job with some printing thrown in, and it paid $120 a week full time. It was good enough for me. I decided I wanted to save $1500, and then adios New York, hola San Francisco Bay Area. United Feature Syndicate was a gas. The job lasted from January until May 1973. I took the train every day from the Scarsdale station, and hung out at my cousin Carla's every Tuesday night, hitting the East Side bar scene. I took piano and guitar lessons, went to the local Y once a week to play racquetball or basketball, and took a psychology course at SUNY Purchase one night a week. The class was fun and stimulating. In fact, while living at home, I ended up garnering a total of 13.5 units of credit from SUNY-Purchase, which made me feel like I was heading towards graduation, even if

I had a long way to go. All the classes were in psychology, or social psychology, or the philosophy of psychology. Dad and I took the first one together, which was not too bad. In my fifteen months in New York, I was pretty busy. Busy, but mostly having fun. Particularly the last nine months of it, after my return from Columbus, and the dreary, disheartening visit with Carole.

By January of 1973, Carole, my sweetie from Columbus, had become a somewhat distant memory, until she called me up one night to let me know she had landed in the psych unit at OSU, Upham Hall, and asked if I would visit her. With no hesitation, given her undying loyalty, dedication, and devotion to me in my time of need, I hopped on a plane and spent two days with her, providing support, encouragement, and love. It was hard to see her so tense and anxious. But she had been through an abortion, had been smoking too much pot, and was overburdened with school and her family's ongoing difficulties. It all had been a bit too much. Plus, her experience with me and my crack-up had taken a cumulative toll on her mental health. I felt sad and a bit guilty, but glad to be able to be of help to her. I was glad that the shoe was on the other foot for a change, and that I was the helper rather than the helpee.

Yet at the same time, a part of me didn't think of us as a couple. The part with gonads. Thus, in the evening, I found my buds Paul and John, my riot mates, and once again we were hitting the streets, looking for women. Carole gradually felt better, returned to school, and finished up the quarter. She had good recuperative powers. I returned to New Rochelle and resumed my duties at my new job at United Feature Syndicate. The timing was perfect. I printed out copy for feature writers like Jack Anderson, which gave me a three-day leg up on the public, newswise, so I got some scoops on what was happening during the Watergate scandal, which was heating up big time. Between printing by day, and Roger Grimsby, Bill Beutel and Geraldo Rivera at night on WABC TV local news, I was politically informed, in detail. I read "On the Road," the Kerouac classic, and "The Family," by Ed Sanders, about Charles Manson, and "Dharma Bums," also by Kerouac, as prep for my move to California. The impression I got from these books is that there were many disparate elements operating in California, a bucolic, natural, warm, outdoorsy, spiritual, radical scene, filled with rebellious, anarchic souls. And I guess the dark offshoot of this was the drug-addled, angry, Hells Angels, cultish, L. Ron Hubbard and bloody Chuck Manson side of the fence. Monterey and Altamont. I was intrigued and chastened by the info, but undeterred. The Bay Area would be my home as soon as I got my stake together.

Fifteen weeks was all that it took. Saving $80 a week added up to a grand total of $1200 bucks. My old man threw in another six for an even total of $1800. By May 1, I was financially ready, but not before I had some more adventures in Boston, Washington, and Purchase. Boston consisted of seeing high school friends Rick and Mac for weekend fun on two occasions. Washington DC consisted of another high school friend, Mark, and another New Rochelle friend Ken Cacase. We drove down and caught a lot of music and partying at the Cellar Door in Georgetown. We caught Oscar Brown, Jr., a jazzy, bluesy singer. Then, there was the last episode of note, which happened at Purchase about three weeks before leaving for California. On a Tuesday night in April, unseasonably warm, I headed up to Purchase to finalize the grades I had received in my psych classes, and to consolidate the transcripts from OSU and Purchase for later usage. Upon getting this done, I encountered the Dean of Arts and Humanities, an astute, perceptive man named Arnold, just like my namesake. We began drinking, and somehow, for the fourth time in four years, I allowed myself to get involved in a homosexual encounter. This was the first one with a white guy; the other three had been with Black guys. One was from my freshman dorm, one from the football team my sophomore year, and the last I met on High Street in Columbus, who, under the guise of us getting stoned, put DMT in some grass without my knowledge. I found myself tripping my brains out and had a dick in my ass before I know what hit me. I think that this experience, this rape, for lack of a better word, taught me a lesson, as I was not turned on by this stuff. But this Arnold guy was a smooth operator, and after a few beers I somehow began letting him jerk me off, before I recoiled in revulsion and disgust, and fled. This would turn out to be my last foray in homosexual experimentation, as I had now convinced myself, via experience, that it was women that turned me on. Actually, it had always been that way, but I was still interested in experimenting. In retrospect, I don't know why. But I was always looking to explore the edge. First, gambling, then cigarettes, then the track, then marijuana, then acid, then gay sex, then radical politics. A lot of dabbling. Playing the edge. I was bored by the conventional ways of doing things, and the conventional things that conventional people do. Always in search of new forms of excitement, I rarely thought things through before I did them, and was often driven by my low tolerance for boredom. It got me into trouble, but also served as an avenue for unusual, often interesting adventures. But this last thing, with this guy Arnold, had me a bit traumatized. I felt exploited as a student, by an administrator, but also down on myself for allowing it. Whatever. In three weeks I would be out of New Rochelle, I said to myself. I tried not to think about this stupid encounter. It mostly worked. My mind was on California.

My last day on the job was April 24, 1973. Saying goodbye to workmates, I headed to the AAA auto store to get a triptych for my cross country extravaganza. The triptych's map plan had me going from New Rochelle, to Columbus, to Madison, to the Dells in Wisconsin, to South Dakota, to the Badlands, to Mt. Rushmore, and on to Cheyenne, Wyoming, then finally Denver. Then on to Bryce and Zion National Parks in Utah, to Albuquerque, to Santa Fe, to Tucson, to the Grand Canyon, then back to Denver, to Yellowstone and the Grand Tetons, to Montana, to Idaho, and into Canada. First, British Columbia, then Vancouver, then Jasper, Banff, Lake Louise, and Revelstoke, and then back to Vancouver, and down to Seattle, and into Portland, and down the Pacific Coast highway into Mendocino, and finally, on Saturday, June 23, 1973, landing in Berkeley, coming off the University Avenue exit off highway 80 heading west on a beautiful Saturday morning at noon. There, I would immediately head to the apartment of my friend from OSU, Hal Bartel. But I digress. I was getting ahead of myself. I hadn't even left yet. This was only the game plan. But it was very concrete and specific. And it would start tomorrow.

CHAPTER 3

You Can't keep a Good Man Down, But You Can Try

Duffel Bag in tow, cigarettes and triptych in hand, I was ready. But before I left on the first of May, I had a sweet parting with my Dad. He was reconciled that I was leaving, having given his blessing, even though he had mixed feelings given that I was going to no job and had no college degree. He described my move as, "my royal road to romance." An ambiguous statement if I ever heard one. It sounded like Dad's effort to make the best of his twenty-three year old's desires and lack of direction. But he also knew he was powerless to do anything about it. I had money, a car, and I'd rehabilitated myself, and so his task as a father, after what seemed like much reflection, something he was not used to doing a lot of, was to find a way to give his blessing and put a positive spin on my decision to head west. "The Royal Road to Romance." A journey into the unknown. I was mostly excited. Not prone to feeling much fear - counter-phobic, they call it. I was relishing the opportunity.

Even though it had been seven years since I first hatched the dream, better late than never.

The four years since my departure at the IOL in Hartford, nut house number 1, followed by a sputtering, checkered career as a college student at Ohio State, including a crushing break up at the hands of my first love and high school sweetheart Marla, followed by a massive campus protest, riots, jail and assorted hijinks, followed by dropping out of OSU, to temporary exile in Madison, Wisconsin to regain my bearings, followed by the death by lung cancer of my sweet gentle mother, too soft and self-effacing for this world. This was all followed by finding another great love, Carole. This, in turn, was followed by the return of more mania, and another long hospitalization in Columbus.

Back to New York, and yet another attempt at mental and vocational rehabilitation, and then patched up again, and well enough to resume a normal life. But now, as I take my leave on May 1, after bidding goodbye to my oldest bud, Rick, in Cambridge, and my gambling, drugs, sports, and Greenwich Village music high school road dogs Mac, Mark, and Kenny, I am officially ready to begin my adulthood. I play the Beach Boys, who belt out, "On my way to Sunny California. On my way to spend another Sunny Day." Cat Stevens sings, "I got my freedom, I can make my own rules, oh yeah, the ones that I choose." Many psychic knockdowns. I have taken my proverbial mandatory eight counts, shaken it off, cleared my head, and despite all of these slings and arrows, I was still standing, motherfuckers. That's right. Still standing. I WAS JUST GETTING STARTED. On the road, heading to Columbus to see Carole, my only company for the next ten hours would be the FM radio until I was out of range, and then back to AM. The last night in NYC with Mark and Kenny, and visiting Max's Kansas City, had given me a preview of the direction the counter culture was taking. Especially in New York. Glam rock. The truth was, it had me freaked out. I thought of it as gay, cross-dressing, androgynous stuff. As a radical, and most importantly, on an emotional level, being for the underdog, in my mind I knew it was not right to cast aspersions on any discriminated group. But on another level, I felt revulsion. I had been raped by a man, and I had some residual anger for what I'd been through. I had wanted to get that man away from me, but I had been vulnerable. I was stoned on DMT and dependent on this man for my sanity until I came down. This memory made me recall an earlier episode that happened when I was fifteen. I had gotten lost in the Moscow subway while on a tour with my parents, and was confused by the Greek lettering, being unable to speak or read Russian. I asked a gay dude for help finding my parents.. He spoke Russian and English, this man who befriended me on the Moscow streets. I felt forced to be nice to those gay dudes on both occasions in order to regain my bearings. This Glam Rock thing had me freaked out, and now it was all over the FM. When I listened to it, my immediate response was to get freaked out, scared. The easy solution to avoiding glam rock in my Toyota as I hit Plainfield, New Jersey on highway 80, was to simply flip the station, which I did often. I liked songs like "Ground Control to Major Tom" and "All the Young Dudes." I just didn't like the feelings they evoked in me. Flipping the station produced other songs which triggered other memories or feelings. Some, much more pleasant, reminded me of my days with Marla, or some other girl from high school. Folk and folk rock were much more evocative of my college days. This is how I got to Columbus in seemingly no time. By 11:30pm I was at Carole's door on a muggy, hot Columbus night in the middle of the week. Carole was in school, still finishing up her Masters in Special Ed, on her way to becoming a teacher of the developmentally disabled. She was glad to see me, a little tired from studying, but offered me a beer as we stayed up talking and hugging for an hour or so, and then got into bed where we made love for the first time in nine months. It was a sweet affair, as Carole and I really loved each other. More importantly, we understood each other. It was easy to be with her, as it was for her to be with me. Carole had also recently had a trip to the nuthouse back in February, at OSU's Upham Hall, the psych facility, where she checked in for acute anxiety, panic attacks, and depression. Now she seemed fine, was off meds and back to school, and even relatively happy, for her. She had a morose and anxious side that could dominate her personality, but that night it was mostly sweetness and glee. Carole was a dirty blonde, 5'1" Clevelander from Garfield Heights with a great body. But not haughty. If anything, she was a little shy, which I found appealing. She was bright and we shared similar interests: psychology, politics, music, and existential philosophy. We got each other. It was great.

I was there to see her and my two male buddies. Everyone else I know from my OSU days had either graduated and gone, or dropped out and gone, except for these two dudes, John Flowers and Paul Ricciardo. They were my running buddies from the riots, who I'd been friends with ever since. Since the second part of my sophomore year, the year of the riots, spring of 1970, they had been my main consistent friends. Carole and I were tight. She was living with a roommate on south campus. We were both medication free. Drug free, mostly, notwithstanding beer and a little weed now and then. No weed for Carole. She was sensitive to it. It made her anxious, and occasionally paranoid. She rarely had a good time. Same with me, mostly. Carole had an alcoholic father, who was soft and sweet to her, but unreliable and wussy with his wife, a shrewish pushy lady toward Carole and her Dad. Carole couldn't stand her. It was clear we were still in love. It was clear we got along great. It was clear we got each other. But there was one thing that wasn't so clear. Where would we be together? I was California dreamin'. Carole wanted to stay in Ohio with me, get married, have kids, settle down and make a life together. Immediatamente. I was like, no way Jose. Too young. Too many wild oats. Guess we were in two different places. Too bad. I had never met anyone who came close in so many important ways. Values, interests, attraction, sack work, fun. We definitely would have made it work. But Carole was just not ready to leave Ohio and be with me in California. And vice versa.

We spent a bittersweet week in Ohio. My time was mostly with her, and occasionally hanging out with Paul or John, both separately and together, usually at Larry's, the OSU hippie bar. Paul, my radical running buddy and comedy partner, had graduated with a degree in poli sci, directionless. Not really working, he was low level pot dealing. John, a little older, about twenty-six, was on the verge of getting his degree in business. He was a Columbus local, not going anywhere. In Larry's Bar with Carole and Paul one night, I ran into Jim Kuhl. Since I saw him last in 1971, he suffered a serious motorcycle accident and lost the use of his left arm. Jim and I got to talking, and he asked me about my trip. It turned out he had some former OSU, politico friends I knew who were living in Denver. One of my stops. Jim assured me we would have a place to stay so I invited him to come with me. He was affable and we had enough in common, so we made a plan for May 8, first via Madison to see my two brothers Dave and Lew, then on to the Badlands, Black Hills, Wyoming and Denver. Jim Kuhl was cool. Haha. I saw him every night in Larry's after that, with Carole or Paul or John. With John and I, the thing was cruising women and talking about race and music. With Paul, politics and women were the bill of fare.

With Carole, I covered a wide-ranging set of topics. Family (hers and mine), psychology, race relations, feminism, gay liberation, eating organically, the environmental movement, how to raise kids, and music. We had a lot in common, including a pretty strong attraction, a shared set of values, interest in drugs (pot and acid), a desire to change the world, and an anti-war, pro-Black Power point of view. She and I, not to mention Paul and John, had come through the riots together the previous year. Carole had noticed me during the riots and christened me Little Yippie because I hung out with a taller guy who also wore a bandanna, who she called Big Yippie. She saw me give my famous oval speech to 10,000 demonstrators, haranguing the Jewish kids for not giving enough money to bail out arrested demonstrators. She had admired me from afar even though she had an on-again-off-again boyfriend sophomore year. She was my age. Paul was twenty-four, and John Flowers was twenty-six. John had already had a tour of duty in VietNam. Paul, from Pepper Pike in Cleveland, was a suburban kid like myself, and a poli sci major. John was a business major. I was a college dropout, interested in majoring in sociology, who didn't have enough credits accumulated to declare. The week went by fast. Jim Kuhl and I made plans to meet on the 8th of May. It was great to see the three of them, but I felt a bit forlorn, albeit very excited about the upcoming adventure.

The last night with Carole was bittersweet. She was clear about her position, but intrigued and interested about the possibility of coming to northern California. I was clear as well. In my three years in Columbus, I'd pretty much had my fill of the place. Not enough going on, although the people were great. The landscape was too flat and uninteresting. Culturally, it was thin. I was ready. Carole and I spent the last night making love. We went for breakfast at Charburt's the next day, the local greasy spoon. All packed up, I said goodbye, not knowing at the time that it would be the last time I ever saw her. Jim Kuhl was waiting with a knapsack at Larry's, right outside on the street. He threw his stuff into the trunk with my stuff, and we were off.

The West is the Best (May-June 1973) Cols to Madison: May 8, 1973

Jim and I drove to Madison in about eight hours, passing through Indianapolis into Chicago, then the homestretch into Madison. We arrived at Dave Brucher's apartment in the early evening. Dave and Cherise greeted us and took us to Ella's, the local legendary deli. Dave and Cherise were both grad students. Dave, a French history student emphasizing 19th and 20th century cultural and intellectual history. Cherise was a fourth-year student in English, focused on the 19th century female English writers Emily Bronte, Charlotte Bronte, and George Sand. Dave was in his fifth and last year, writing his thesis on a French intellectual of the 20s and 30s, a pacifist named Roman Rolland. He was famous in Dave's mind for his relationship with Sigmund Freud. Freud, in fact, directed some of his book, *Civilization and its Discontents*, against the pacific thinking of Rolland. In particular, he railed against Rolland's belief

in an "oceanic state" as a desired state. Rolland was an early propo-
nent of eastern philosophy, particularly Hinduism. Freud was highly
critical of the oceanic state as a desired goal. Rather, he saw it as a
regression to the womb state with the mother. Freud, it seemed to
me at the time, was overly realistic, or pessimistic - even negative
about the possibilities of transcendence. Anyway, it was Rolland,
and increasingly Freud, who dominated Dave's intellectual interests,
while Cherise, an avowed feminist by this time, studied and wrote
about nineteenth century English women writers, because she saw
them as forerunners of women's liberation, which of course, was
now in full swing.

Jim Kuhl and I, while professing our allegiance to the new
women's movement in part because we were sympathetic to any
movement that had underdog status in American society, also wanted
to get laid. So strategically, this was the time of the development of
the sensitive male. If this was the persona one had to assume to get
laid, so be it. Freud was right in that way. The goal of life was to
get laid, or pleasure seeking. This may be a fairly crude reading of
Freud, but to me, at least accurate in its essence. I'm big on essences
in my thinking.

Dave and Cherise put us up. Lew, my younger brother, finishing
his freshman year, joined us for dinner at the Deli. The conversation was lively, centering on politics, movies, and literature, with an
occasional smattering of sports thrown in, primarily between Lew
and me. The political discourse amongst the four of us went back
and forth between very abstract political theory, including Marx
and Max Weber, about whose philosophies Dave and Cherise knew
the most, but most often switching to the political situations of the
day; the Watergate hearings, Nixon, the New Left response, the
Weathermen, and the latest from the Black Power movement. The

fact that I was moving to the Bay Area focused things on radical politics, the Free Speech Movement, and the Black Panther party, but also student politics at Madison, and similarities and differences with Berkeley. Dave was heavily into Freud at this point, but not having been in therapy, not to mention four rounds of hospitalizations, his talk lacked the authenticity and precision that I brought to the understanding of the therapeutic process. Not to mention my major competitive juice with the dude in just about everything. With Lew, it was different. I had practically raised him, and didn't feel competitive with him. Although, with Lew being the youngest, the feeling might not have been mutual but I didn't think about our relationship in that way, only that we were close and that it felt basically easy and fun. Between Dave and Lew, there was a nine-year age difference. A big brother little brother situation. Lew could feel put off. Dave could be pedantic, condescending, patronizing. Then again, Dave could feel dismissed, disrespected, and put off by the two of us. Especially me in some ways, because I was closer in age. I could be contentious and blunt - go for the jugular. I lacked diplomatic skills, but luckily, comedy, humor and joke-making leavened the contact, making the aggressive feelings more palatable. Cherise seemed to enjoy the combat, both watching it and being a participant. I always felt her support in these situations, and in one-on-one encounters as well. She liked Lew as well, but didn't have as close a relationship probably, because of the gap in age. So there we were that night in what passed for Madison's version of a Jewish deli. Jim Kuhl was an amused observer and occasional participant, particularly when the conversation turned to politics, or the differences between Madison and Columbus, the city and the school. Ohio State clearly won in the sports department, and possibly weather. Both had rather severe winters, Madison much worse. A lot more days in the below zero realm. Summers, both cities sucked for my money, and actually that was the consensus. Humidity central. Politically and academically Wisconsin won hands down. Again, the consensus. Drugs were about the same, with the exception being Columbus was known as the Quaalude capital of the world, which they were due to it being the home base of Rorer, the manufacturers of Quaaludes. We in Columbus called quaaludes sopers. Short for soporifics. Jim Kuhl and I regaled our Badger mates about the scene on High Street on any given Friday or Saturday night. There, you could see any number of undergraduates and locals reeling on the sidewalks from the effects of the ludes, especially when combined with alcohol. A potentially lethal combination. Madison was definitely more beautiful, with its two lakes, Mendota and Menota. Between the five of us, there was consensus, and little if any friction about any of these topics. The only time it got at all dicey was when Cherise brought up inevitable feminist issues about the power inequality on the job front and the division of labor inequality on the home front. We men all knew she was right, and basically agreed, but nevertheless, she made me squirm, because I knew I was not the most ideal practitioner or partner in the desired goal of egalitarian relationships. Better perhaps in my empathy and agreement about the need for parity and equality of opportunity and pay on the work front. There, at least so far, I felt less threatened.

Madison was a pleasure. But after three days or so, it was time to shove off. Leaving Dave and Cherise's apartment on Monday after a relaxing and fun weekend, the journey was to truly begin. No more stops to visit lovers and family, at least for me. For Jim, Denver beckoned. From here on in, I would be driving into the unknown. Next stop, the Dells, Wisconsin's favorite state resort.

Nothing much to look at for the two of us. We were after bigger bear. "The West is the best. Follow us. We'll do the rest." Jim Morrison's solemn dictum was, by this time, heavily ingrained in my psyche, and left a stain of intolerance for anything less than the spectacular, which I had been fantasizing about since the mid 60s. Soon, that red Toyota Corona, with me behind the wheel, and one-armed Jim next to me in the shotgun seat was itching to get past the predictable midwest. Finally, we arrived in South Dakota, with more prairie monotony, until Jim saw a familiar sight. Two hitchhikers of the hippie variety on Highway 90. A white dude with straggly, black, shoulder-length hair, dirty black jeans, brown boots, equally dirty if not just dusty, and his compadre, a Black dude with a huge western cowboy hat made of brown felt. Jim barked at me, "Hey, let's pick these guys up. We've got room." Without hesitation, I stopped the Corona about twenty feet past the two scraggly hitchhikers, and watched with amusement as they ran towards our car and got into our backseat, with smallish backpacks in tow. The Black guy's name was Steve, while the white guy called himself Vic. They were both from Bloomington, Indiana. And they too were on their way to the West Coast. No particular part, just as long as it was the Pacific Coast. We informed them of our immediate destination, Denver, but also talked up the idea that we would be heading first into the badlands of South Dakota, the black hills of South Dakota, then Cheyenne, Wyoming until finally our final end point, Denver. They were eager and enthusiastic, and let it be known almost from the start that they would go as far as we were comfortable traveling with them. Well, this turned out to be all the way to Denver, but not before we had some rip-roaring adventures.

Vic was a funny dude. I felt outnumbered as the only easterner among three other midwesterners, but Vic and I provided the wry, sarcastic quips. Raised on TV, as we all were, it was no stretch to immediately go into our best Western drawls from thousands of hours watching Westerns on tv and at the movies. For Jim, Steve and Vic, being from the Midwest, it was no stretch to go from those flat folksy tones into out and out southern drawls once we hit the Badlands. We got our practice a little before coming into Mitchell, South Dakota, the home of the beloved Democratic candidate for president in 1972, George McGovern. Mitchell was not how I would have pictured it, or to put another way, George McGovern was not an accurate representation of this rather hick town in the middle of nowhere. We entered the town on a Sunday morning. The town was basically deserted. Everyone was in church or nursing a hangover. Whatever. The four of us were dusty, dirty, hippiesque characters headed into Ada's Cafe at 8 am. Hungry. Using our best western slang, talking about dry gulching and bushwhacking, the four of us, including the Black dude, were probably pretty exotic to the waitress, a fifty-five-year-old gray-haired lady, thin as a rail.

She offered, "What are you boys having today?"

We opted for bacon and eggs, and French toast. So far, all was well. Some slight weirdness. Midwestern church station on the radio. Not too bad. But just then, as the four of us were drinking our coffee and waiting for our breakfast, and shooting the shit in western slang, in walked a fucking cowboy. With chaps and spurs. I swear to God. As we were the only ones in the joint, the four of us looked at each other, amazed at the sight and trying not to laugh, trying to control ourselves at the weird, yet quite American sight we were seeing, our efforts at composure not holding out. After thirty seconds, the four of us exploded in paroxysms of uncontainable laughter, the coffee spraying out of our respective mouths. We thought we were going to be killed. But fortunately, neither the waitress nor the cowboy paid us any mind.

We escaped with our lives. At least that time. A prelude to the splendor of our entrance into the west. For me, for us, it was the Badlands. Mile upon mile of bare rock formations, sparse, barren land that gave off an eerie, otherworldly vibe. There was total agreement amongst the four of us. We played cowboys and Indians in the barren land, looking for rocks to hide behind in order to either bushwhack or dry gulch the other team. Vic and me vs. Jim and Steve. Vic and I were the cowboy bandits, Steve and Jim, the Sioux Indian tribe in pursuit. Periodically, Vic or I would surprise the Sioux braves and dry gulch them and take them prisoner. You could say we bushwhacked them. I don't really know the difference. Regardless, we had a blast. Camping out in the Black Hills, we did not meet Rocky Racoon. But, we did meet a babe named McGill, who called herself Lil. Actually, everyone knew her as Nancy. Anywho, enough of the Beatles White Album. Back to camping.

We ate burgers, dogs, and beans. We did not drink Coors beer. There was a boycott going on with them, as they were union busters, and very right wing. We drank Rolling Rock, or settled for Bud. Burgers, beans, beer, and trying not to Bogart that joint, around the campfire. Quiet, not too many campers, this time of year. A splendid time was had by all. More Beatles.

The next day, off to Rushmore, also in the Black Hills, where the presidents rest in a rounded contour of granite and mica. There was a bigger crowd here on this perfect, sunny day. Cerulean sky. No clouds. Vic, Steve, Jim and I continue to dick around, even at such a sacred American site as Rushmore. It was downright sacrilege from Vic, and somewhat Steve, although he was much more careful than the other three of us, which I chalked up to less his personality, and more his

Blackness. Either way, the dude was careful. Vic and I were the most irreverent. Jim Kuhl, while a nice guy, was basically a serious guy, and although not quite a drag, brought little to the plate entertainment-wise. And for me, on this trip, entertainment was everything. I was into having fun and feeling good. I paid my motherfuckin' dues. Cuatro hospitalizations in five years. I'd be damned if I wasn't gonna have a good time. And this reporter was not gonna let anything or anyone stop my ass. And so no one did. Jim Kuhl was cool. Mostly quiet. I figured he was this way as a result of losing that arm a year ago. Serious shit. Not able to get employment, he was collecting SSI and trying to figure out what he was gonna do next, I guess. This trip was providing that opportunity to get some space, distance from Columbus, or Cumblowus, as I started to call it in my later years. And though Jim talked of it very little, I could tell it was on his mind in the way he talked to Vic and Steve and me. What could a one-armed college graduate with a degree in Agronomy do? Well at least dude had his degree. By the way, what is Agronomy? As for Earl and Stev, I don't think school or career was much on their minds. Their bill of fare was having fun and seeing the sights of this great country of ours. Hippie style.

Well, after an hour of Teddy, George, Thomas and Abe, the four of us were ready to head to the next vista, Cheyenne. The Judy Collins song rang in my head as we headed towards Wyoming, the one from "Who Knows Where the Time Goes," that album from 1968, in my opinion, one of her greatest. Her other two were from 1966 and 1967. "In My Life" featured Judy singing Suzanne, and then in 1967, "Wildflowers," with Both Sides Now, All I Ask, and Michael from Mountains, the album that helped put Joni Mitchell on the map. But I was thinking about her piano-driven song, which was a tribute to her dad. "My Father."

"My Father always promised us that we would live in France."

Yeah, that one. It had that line. "All my sisters soon were gone to Denver and Cheyenne. Marrying their grown-up dreams; the lilacs and the lamb." I had songs up the yin yang, it seemed. For every occasion. And this occasion was no different. So Judy was on the inner turntable as we headed south from the Black Hills down to Cheyenne, and then our final destination, Denver, Colorado.

Big Sky country. Now we were doing it. I was little scared because of Wyoming's rep for not taking too kindly to hippies. I didn't know about the rest of the crew, but I approached Cheyenne with some degree of trepidation. Fortunately, my fears, as usual, were over-blown. People were polite, friendly, helpful, even sweet. The four of us decided on Chinese food, and so we hit the best Chinese restaurant in Cheyenne that evening. At six pm it was still light out. Blue skies. Clear. Huge land expanse. Impossible not to feel good here. We were all feeling good.

Despite the paranoia, folks here treated us with respect. We were polite. We had dough. All was well. Neither politics nor religion ever came up in patter with waitresses, store clerks or bank tellers. But we were eager to go to Denver, so after a surprisingly good Chinese dinner with not bad Wonton soup, chicken chow mein, and fortune cookies, we four headed to the Toyota. That cherry red short had been doing the job. Hummed like a baby. Never broke down. Jim prepped me on who was in Denver and who we expected to stay with. Denver would be adios for Steve and Vic as they headed for the coast. Probably Monterey and the Big Sur Area. We would be hanging out in Denver for a while, then take a side trip to New Mexico, Albuquerque, and Tucson, and then south Utah (Zion and Bryce canyons to be exact). Then Jim would take a greyhound back to Columbus while

I continued my journey to the Grand Tetons, Yellowstone and parts northwest. But first, there was still plenty of fun to be had in Denver.

Jim and I knew a lot of the same people from the Third World Solidarity Group, Ohio State's version of SDS, after it broke up into two groups: Progressive Labor, and Weathermen. From 1969-1972, the two of us were involved in numerous demonstrations, pickets, boycotts, and of course the big one: the 1970 riots, which is really when we met for the first time. In Denver we would stay with George Bohichik, his moll Lena, a co-leader of TWSG, Bernie Donenberg, the fiery orator on campus on Kent State Day, and Steve Stein. Steve and Bernie had been the co-leaders of SDS prior to its break up in 1969, and had exited Columbus after the riots to an encampment in Denver. Here they were leading a mostly hippie existence. Menial jobs, organic eating and food growing, and a lot of dope smoking. Maybe dealing a little. Nice people. Mellow. But sharp, politically.

The ride to Denver went by quickly. We bid adieu to our two hitchhiker buddies, Vic and Steve, wished them well, and then headed to Bernie and Steve's house on Larrimore Street, the same Larrimore Street where none other than the great Neal Cassady grew up, and which served as one of the locales in Kerouac's "On the Road." The area was kind of rundown and industrial. However, we were close to parks, and most importantly, there were girls living in the house. Bonnie and Katy. A redhead and a dirty blonde, both with thick wavy hair and blue eyes. Bernie and Steve were dark haired with full beards. Bernie in a ponytail, and Steve with a long Jew-fro. We spent our days going to the park, getting stoned, listening to music, and walking the dogs. At night there were gatherings at their place, and elsewhere. The highlight was going to visit Lena in Nederland, an old mining town up in the Rockies.

Lena was holed up there with a bunch of refugees, bandidos and politicos on the lamb for various nefarious activities. Living in a town surrounded by majestic mountains with sweeping vistas, she seemed ecstatic. But Lena always seemed ecstatic, even in her old Columbus hippie radical days. Only now, she wasn't leading demonstrations or running action planning meetings. Just living the life. Hanging out, getting stoned, waitressing in the local restaurant tavern. Seemed idyllic. She and George were broken up so she was footloose and fancy free. Katy and Bonnie were free as well, and mostly around while Jim and I were there, both before we took off New Mexico, and after we returned. I made my forays and inquiries with both Bonnie and Katy if you must know, reprobate that I was. I didn't get much of a bite. Oh well. As for Lena, on the days we went up there to hang with her, I never thought of her as a possibility. She wasn't my type. Too hostile, or critical or something. Of course, now she was heavily into the feminist and gay liberation thing. But not so heavily that she might refuse the advances of some handsome, interesting, clean man. The highlight for Jim and I in Nederland was less the people and more the scenic magnificence of the place. Neither Jim nor I could get over the massive blue skies, majesty of the mountain range, and most importantly, the way the town was enveloped in this cave-like setting. We spent a lot of time looking up. If you wanted to look down, you had to drive or hike up into the Rockies to get the big-time vistas. I liked it visually both ways. Actually, over the eight days we were there, I mostly spent my time in a state of wow from the beauty of it all. But restless souls that we were, and prisoners of our schedule, even though we were having a great time with Steve and Bernie, and even old abrasive Lena, we were committed to New Mexico, Arizona, and Utah. Terrible dilemma!

When we hopped back into Mr. Red Octopus, my new nickname for the Toyota Corona, Albuquerque wasn't far. Luckily, I knew someone there, Richie Young, one of Marla's best male friends from high school, and the only New Rochelle male besides me that went to her wedding. One of the great mistakes of all time. Anyway, at that time, Richie had invited me to come visit him in Albuquerque. So I guessed now was as good a time as any. I called him when we reached the outskirts. Luckily, he was here, and enthusiastic about me and Jim coming over, and so with that green light, we made our way to Richie's house, where we proceeded to go out to a fine barbecue place. We shared BBQ beef, Bud and stories of college and for Richie, and my continued contact with Marla. Believe it or not, after four years of breakup, a one month long tease about getting together, one surprise visit, and my masochistic appearance at her wedding, and despite being with many other girls at this point, despite being in a major relationship with Carole for two years, despite all that, I was still carrying a torch for Marla. I knew in my heart that she wasn't right for me, as she was not on the same wavelength politically, intellectually, or religiously, but despite all of that, I still hurt for her. Maybe it was because we never slept together. Maybe, it was because she was my first love. Maybe, it was because of her undying love, devotion and loyalty to me during my illness. Whatever it was, that ache in my heart was still present. And I had a masochistic need to know how she was. Richie was not psychologically astute or sensitive enough to stop me before filling me in. She was fine. Graduated from Emory. Married. Husband in his last year of medical school. Waitressing in Atlanta. Sounded happy. Did my name come up? Richie replied actually it did, during the *how are the kids in New Rochelle doing* part of the talk. Richie and I talked at length that night about Marla. In some ways he knew her better than me. As they were just friends, he got to know her without the sexual piece, which distorts what one can see. From Richie's perspective, she was great. Fun loving, good dancer, kind of straight. She smoked a little dope, but really had conventional interests and values. Since being with her husband, she had become more religious, and gotten involved in Hillel, and interested in Israel. Richie told me that Marla's younger sister had moved to Israel to finish college and settle there. Marla now had great interest and passion for Israel, and it turned out her parents did too, along with her husband Saul, who I thought was bordering on being a zealous Zionist Ob/Gyn. I was jealous, but masked it in some bullshit hippie lingo like calling him a straight neck, or even worse a sellout. I felt anyone not living an alternative lifestyle in those days was a sellout. I bought into the counterculture trip, lock, stock and barrel. Unbeknownst to me, it served as a convenient rationale for my own lack of success, and provided a cultural, political cover to go after anyone who had gained a margin of success, particularly Marla's husband, whom I had only met once, and of course, despised. My own pathology. But hey, in 1973 I was in good company. A lot of middle class kids had dropped out, or, having finished college, were living marginal existences and espousing hippie or alternative beliefs, like smoking dope, anger at the man, underground rock, and the whole dichotomized world view of hip and straight. They are wrong, we are right. They are uptight. We are cool. They are conservative or conventionally liberal. We are radical. They live in houses. We live in cooperatives, collectives, communes. A great cover. Only it only partially worked. But at that moment, in 1973, in Albuquerque, New Mexico, talking to Richie Young about Marla and her husband provided me with succor and self-righteous belief in my rightness. Afterall, I was off to Berkeley, the epicenter of all things radical, hip and alternative. Fuck her, fuck her husband. And yet, the pain was still present, a narcissistic injury incurred because I had been broken up with.

Richie was good for a night, and then it was time to head west to Winslow, and Prescott, Arizona, and then up into the canyons of Bryce and Zion in Utah. As we approached the park at Zion, the road grew narrow, with deep golden-green caverns on both sides. Jim and I searched for a place to camp. We found one outside of camp. And, after quickly lighting a fire, burning some smokies, and boiling a can of beans over the fire, we hit the sack almost immediately. We had the whole campground, as it was the middle of the week, and not that crowded. There was not a lot of noise in the place, with mostly older people, and we knew their drill, asleep early, just like us. The next day we hit the narrows, the main attraction at Zion, a narrow inlet between two canyons that had to be hiked in with frequent treks into the water. But the water was never too deep, knee-high at worst. Another blast as Jim and I were high again. Although Jim liked to augment the feeling with pot, I didn't. After another night of camping, we moved on to more amazement at the orangey, stalagmite and stalactite-shaped expanse of a mountainous canyon called Bryce. In some ways, Bryce was even more spectacular because of its otherworldly vibe, the surreal yet strange, serene beauty we hiked in, luxuriating on a perfect blue-sky day, crisp fresh air amidst a sea of orange and burnt sienna rock. Another ecstatic day in nature. The fucking West was the best.

We headed back to Denver the next morning. There, Jim and I bid adieu, as he would be heading east back to Columbus, via Greyhound, and I would be heading north and then west into the Grand Tetons, Yellowstone, Montana, Idaho, and then into Canada and Vancouver. Jim and I had had a successful trek together. Pretty much conflict free, we enjoyed mellow vibes the whole way with our hippie hitchhiker friends and our SDS hosts in Denver and Nederland, and with Richie, my new Rochelle buddy, despite an angst filled talk about Marla. The final report card: A for vibes, A for adventure. The only bad grade was an F for lack of pussy.

Now I was on my own. Really on my own this time. No hitchhikers or friends, at least for a while. Did I like to be alone? I said I did. I felt like I did a lot of times when I was with other people, people I liked, or even loved. People I found interesting at least some of the time. And yet, on my trip so far, I hadn't been alone at all, except for the ten-hour drive from New Rochelle to Columbus. Other than that, I'd been with Carole, Jim Kuhl, John Flowers and Paul Ricciardo, Dave and Lew. Then the hitchhikers, Steve and Vic. Then Steve, Bernie, and Lena in Colorado. Then Rob in Albuquerque. So I didn't know if this desire to be alone was really true. Maybe it was that I liked to be around other people, but I liked to be LEFT alone after a while. Whatever it was, I was alone now, heading to the Grand Tetons, Wyoming and Yellowstone.

It was not so bad being alone. And yet, now that I was alone, all I could do was think about the people I'd been with, or the people (women) I'd like to meet. My reason for living was back. Women. As Burt Lancaster once said in "The Professionals," one of my favorite western movies from 1966, "Yeah, I need a woman. Any size, any shape, any color." As the local yokels used to say in Columbus, "I was as horny as a two peckered billy goat." Yeah, it was true. I could not, and did not really want to deny it. To myself, or others really. But, let's face it, when it came to women, you really couldn't be too obvious or you got nowhere. You had to be a gentleman, had to act interested in them as people whether you were or not. Luckily for me, I rarely found that a problem. I liked women, mostly. I actually found them more interesting and more honest, at least from the standpoint of admitting vulnerabilities. The only thing they had trouble with was expressing rage. At least, that was true with a lot of them. But, I digress. Here I was, driving on my own for the first time and all I could think of was dames, as Bogie and my father used to say. Ah, what the fuck. Who gives a shit. Really. Put on the radio and get there.

At the Grand Tetons, I found a place to camp, and the next day I went horseback riding through the Tetons. A glorious trek. Unforgettable. Then back in the Corona and off to Yellowstone, this time on a mission even more than usual. In the mode now, I was feeling less desperate, less urgent. I was back in my Cool Hand Luke mode, a good mode for meeting women. They went for that aloof shit. Let them come to me. A winning hand. Particularly with the prettiest types, because the prettiest ones were used to having to fend off the attention of guys, and found it tiresome, and downright annoying, but left to their own devices, would invariably go for the guys who acted disinterested. That was the gambit that I had learned. Don't ask me where or when.

When I arrived in Yellowstone, I headed for the nearest diner for the usual all American meal. Burger, coke and fries. It so happened that I got this really friendly waitress at the counter. She wasn't a local, just working to be at the national park that summer. Her name was Justine and she was from St. Louis. Sweet, friendly, competent. Maybe a little flirty. Hard to tell, we would see. Justine was quick at her work, dispensing her orders with efficiency and a bit of sassy humor, with that unique St. Louis western southern drawl. The place was about half empty at 2:30 in the afternoon. I noticed she kept coming back to my area to fill up my coke with refills and talk. It could be because I was the only long hair in the place at this time, and it could be because I was alone. Whatever it was, I was eating it up. I was fucking horny, man. Ain't had no pussy since Columbus. It seemed like I had ample enough opportunities, but maybe that wasn't true. Maybe my assessment of a lack of interest from the ladies in Madison and Denver was accurate. So stop your bitchin', I told myself, while Justine was taking care of some older customers. Play it cool man, I told myself. Be relaxed, don't come across as too eager or interested, nonchalant wins the day. I was just tired and hungry enough as to where that approach was not that hard to come by, for Justine kept coming back to my counter, asking me about where I was headed, where I had been, where I went to school, was it my first time in Yellowstone. I asked her when she was getting off. She said in an hour, and invited me to go with her to get a firsthand look at Old Faithful. I said great, as she was obviously unattached. Or if she was attached, she was not that attached. All I knew is she was putting out a good vibe. I ate my burger and fries all casual. Paid my bill and told her I'd be back in a half hour.

She smiled and said, "See you soon."

I walked out, and walked into the book store and browsed the books on Yellowstone, and other national parks. Glacier, Yosemite, Tetons. Beautiful pictures, and the place was mostly empty. Pretty soon, the half hour was up, and I headed back to the burger place where Justine had just finished changing into her street clothes.

"Ready?" she inquired.

"Yup," I half-smiled back.

"Okay mister, let's go then," she said, as she pointed with her finger towards the door, and in the direction of Old Faithful, about fifty yards away.

"You ain't gonna believe this. Unbelievable," she gushed. The look, the smell, the heat. It was so cool. She was right. The geyser was dramatic. We watched in silence, and then she asked, "Wanna get high?

"Of course," I replied quickly, almost giving away my intentions. We headed to her rather modest quarters, and sat on her bed, which made up most of the place, along with a hot plate and mini fridge and a narrow bathroom. A studio apartment on a good day. We toked up. It smelled like your basic Mexican grass, not that I'm an expert or anything. She agreed. We pass the j back and forth a few times, then quit. Loins heated up. We looked at each other for a nano-second, and then commenced to go at it. Amen. Like a drunk, I lapped her up. And while it lasted maybe five minutes or so, I felt like I'd come out of the desert. She was passionate, in her way. She asked me if I wanted to stay the night, but that ole "after cum" had kicked in and as politely as I could, I said I had to be moseying. But before I did, I needed to eat something, so I went to a Denny's near the freeway. There, I ran into a long hair named Ted sitting next to me at the counter, where he too was ordering a burger, fries, and a coke. We struck up a conversation about our respective journeys. He was a west coaster from Bellingham, Washington who extolled the virtues of his hometown, another one of those out of the way hippie towns, kind of like Nederland, but not in the mountains. Bellingham was more of a bucolic little town above Seattle, but more central. He strongly encouraged me to stop off there, and gave me the name of his sister Sarah, a divorcee with a small child, who would be happy to put me up at her place, as she was in the habit of being a crash pad for travelers heading up and down the coast. The red-headed brother thought she was a little strange, but assured me Sarah was a nice person. He chalked it up to loneliness, as Sarah's old man up and split once their baby arrived, never to be heard from again. So now Sarah was a single mom having to raise his niece all by herself.

Anyway, Ted insisted it would be fun, maybe even a fringe benefit if she liked me. This was definitely a productive conversation. I put Sarah's number in my wallet, making sure I didn't lose it, as it would come in handy when I came back from Canada, heading south down the coast to my new home, Berkeley. The red-headed dude and I bid adieu, wishing each other safe travel as we headed to our spots. He was on the highway, hitchhiking, heading west. I was back in my trusty Corona, heading north into Montana and places west.

Alone again, I was on my way for the five-hour drive through Big Sky country into Missoula, home of University of Montana, where I happened upon this amazing bar near campus that housed cowboys, Indians and hippies. These three groups were all in the place drinking, mingling, and playing pool, with, as far as I could see, nary a hassle, nary an argument that was not good natured, and nary an altercation. What the fuck was this? Hippie paradise? Everybody was getting along. "Come on people now, smile on your brother," the lyrics to the hippie anthem by the Youngbloods, popped into my brain. They were doing it. But what the hell did I know, I was just going by the surface vibe of things in the present with no knowledge of the inner workings of what the relationships were really like over time. But I was not thinking that way. I was not an anthropologist or ethnologist or social psychologist. I was just a long hair passer through from New York, looking to have a good time, and a good time I was about to have shooting the shit with Rick, the dude sitting next to me, after I got my order of Olympia beer, already my favorite western beer. No way I was drinking that Coors, with their scab labor, anti-union, anti-Chicano attitudes, a corporation run by this dude Adolf Coors, who I heard was a Bircher. Fuck him, fuck his beer. Olympia, please. Thank you.

Yes Rick, I just got here from Yellowstone.

Yes Rick, I've been on the road about 3 plus weeks now.

Yes Rick, I'm from NYC and environs.

Yes Rick, I went to OSU.

Yes, Rick I'm headed for Northern California.

I see, Rick, you're from around here. Oh, you just graduated a year ago from U of M with a degree in Animal Science?

Yes Rick, I do like horses.

No Rick, I never ate moose meat.

No Rick, I ain't never ridden horses freestyle.

No Rick, actually I have never been to or on a ranch.

I see Rick, you live on a ranch with your dad and ranch cattle? Rick, you're sure your old man wouldn't mind having a NY hippie Jew staying out there with you for a few days? Yes Rick, this reporter would love to hang with you there. Yes Rick, let me finish my beer and we'll go. Yes Rick, I'll follow your truck in my car. Ok Rick, it's about a 20 minute ride out of town? Okay, see you there.

Follow I did. I landed in pitch blackness on what appeared to be a big patch of land, smelling of horse manure. Nice smell, that horse manure. I didn't mind sleeping in the barn, and sleep I did, dead to the world until 8:30, when I awoke to the whinnying of horses and bright sunlight. Rick was up, beckoning me to the kitchen for homemade bacon and eggs, pancakes too if I wanted em, coffee, yup. "We'll just have our breakfast, then head out back to the barn. I'll saddle you up with Brick and we'll ride on the ranch all morning. Loping and galloping if you like."

"I like," I told Rick. "Where's your paw," I said, all Opie-like, but not deliberately.

"He's out at the back fence doin' some mendin'. Kind of freaked out when he saw that New York license, and heard you had long hair. Says you can stay one more night then it's adios."

Hmm, I thought to myself. Your basic anti-New York, anti-Semitic mofu. But he called the shots, it was his place. So off riding we went into his gorgeous, mostly gentle terrain. Not too hilly. The horse tuned into my level of competence. I wasn't a complete novice, but not really that proficient either. Brick clicked into me and off we rode, about three hours or so. And man I was fucking saddle sore. We had a beer and some homemade chili made by the Mexican maid, and I was spent. Nap city from 2-5. Rick and I headed into Missoula around six so as to head off any contact with the old man, who was neither happy with his son for my presence on his place, nor probably my existence, if you wanna get right down to it. We hung at the Cowboy, Indian, hippie bar till about 11, listening to the Eagles, Willie Nelson, and Linda Ronstadt on the jukebox. Then it was back to the ranch to crash. I was up around 8:30, and bid Rick adieu and adios motherfuckers. Off to Idaho. Land of the Back to the Landers, survivalist country.

I drove a few more hours after breakfast, and by mid-afternoon, I had to find a place to stay. Sick of camping, I happened upon a logging camp, where for some strange reason, a sign at the entrance to the camps said they don't mind strangers staying there. I arrived again to a barnlike place and a corral, where there was no one but me. Totally quiet. I pulled out my sleeping bag, found a copy of Soldier of Fortune magazine, which I had never seen before, and with its ads for mercenaries, I got scared, thinking holy shit where am I? Still, I slept restfully, but with one eye open, if you know what I mean. I woke up with the sun, and got the fuck out of there before I encountered anyone with a gun.

On to Canada and Vancouver. Good riddance to Idaho. The place gave me the creeps, with its gun culture, and rugged individualist, anti-government, quasi libertarian ethos. Fuck these white people and the horses they rode in on. An hour into the drive, I saw two more hitchhikers are on the road, and once again, I decided to stop on what felt like a momentary whim, or loneliness, or the need for conversation. Whatever it was, we were now three in the Corona again. This time it was two white dudes, Joe and Jack. Both from upstate New York, they were headed to Northern California, one to meet up with the One World Family, a cult lodged in Berkeley that professed peace, love, and harmony, through meditation, vegetarianism, and communal living. The other guy was your basic hippie type, not into much except sex, drugs and rock n' roll. Not hard drugs, just pot. They were nice enough, but I quickly realized that I had made a mistake. It's not like they were dangerous or anything, it's more like they were not that interesting, particularly the spiritual dude who went on and on about Swami Muktananda. Fuck him. I got engaged with the spiritual dude in a mild disagreement regarding world views. He gave me your basic spiritual enlightenment rap that was so popular in countercultural circles, whereas I was your basic this world materialist, mostly of the Marxist variety. The events of the late sixties, and both my observations and participation, had convinced me of that. The ruling class ruled to perpetuate its wealth and power, and mostly through divide and conquer tactics, including dividing the races, the classes and even men and women. That was my trip. Jim had an entirely different view of how the world worked. That the stuff I just described was "maya," or the world of illusion. Seeing we are all one and finding nirvana was the goal in life, and everything else was a waste of time. Society was, is, and always will be both an illusion and a phony power game. On that we could agree. On the causes and solutions we differed. I didn't give a fuck, because it created a dissonance in the car that I wasn't into. Yet I felt a strange commitment, once I picked these guys up, to take them to Vancouver with me. Loneliness was a mofo. Six hours later, we arrived at my old friend Matt Rosen's place in Vancouver. Matt was an old OSU Student Union buddy who I knew from the riots and the aftermath during junior year in 1971. Matt was a sociology major now pursuing a Master's in social work at the University of British Columbia in Vancouver. He lived with his girlfriend, who was also from OSU. Lisa was there when the three of us arrived. Matt was not. He was back in New York visiting family, but Lisa, who knew me, and kind of had an inkling through a letter that I might be coming, was hospitable as hell.

She put us up for a couple of days until I figured out my next move, which, it turned out, would be Jasper, Banff and Lake Louise, three gorgeous turquoise lakes situated on the border between British Columbia and Alberta in the Canadian Rockies. Joe and Jim accompanied me. They weren't so bad. I'd gotten used to Jim by this point. Joe was easy peasy. He just wanted to get stoned and listen to music. Agreeable. I gave Jim my cynical routine enough that he stopped bringing up his spiritual bull shit for a couple of days. This trip was actually pretty pleasant. We hit the turquoise lake magnificence, camped, and ate over a three-day period, including a trip at the end to Revelstoke, a natural hot spring, a place cool to enter into, though not nude, like Esalen in Big Sur, California. It was still fun, though.

Now, after six weeks on the road, I had begun to have enough, so we headed back to Vancouver overnight. Then, I decided I'd had enough of the hitchhikers, and dropped them off the next day in Seattle just before I contacted Sarah, my crash pad contact. I was alone again, and starting to prefer it. People cramped my style. I definitely didn't like to have to relate to people I didn't want to connect with, just because I had a moment of loneliness.

Getting a place to stay was another matter. As the phone picked up on the other end, I heard a sweet-sounding feminine voice with a slight southern drawl that told me to come by, and how to get there. I was there in a jiffy, as it was only about ten minutes from where I was stopped at a truck stop. When I knocked on the door of her flat, slightly outside of town, a brunette who looked a little older than me opened the door to greet me. She showed me where to put my stuff and informed me that she had a little girl, three years old, named Lucy, and asked if I'd like to have dinner with her. She had been told by her Bellingham brother who I met in Yellowstone, that I might be ringing her up, so she wasn't completely surprised by my call. She asked me what my plans are. I told her I was not in any immediate rush, but that I was getting kind of tired of being on the road and was eager to get to Berkeley, my final destination. She nodded in recognition and empathy, understanding my exhaustion from having been on the road for some seven weeks now, even though she could hear in my telling that it had been a good trip in general. She then proceeded to tell me a little bit about her life. She was twenty-six, and her old man left her right after he found out she was pregnant. She grew up in Seattle and graduated from the University of Washington with a degree in psychology. She was going to try to pursue an RN degree as soon as Lucy was old enough to attend kindergarten. In the meantime, she worked part-time as a waitress at the local Denny's, and somewhat sheepishly told me that she was still receiving some financial help from her folks, who still lived in the city. Sarah struck me as a responsible person who loved her daughter and was trying to do right by her. They spent a lot of time together going to parks, meeting up with other moms, and just generally having fun. Lucy liked to draw and do puzzles. She was a vivacious blonde who immediately took a shine to me. I think she was father hungry, as at various times she sat on my lap as if she was hoping I would stay. Sarah seemed to be indicating her own brand of loneliness. She did not communicate anger or resentment towards men, nor did she have an edge. Rather, there was a kind of forlorn sadness about her life, which she tried to mask around Lucy. She had anger towards Glen, Lucy's father, but reserved most of her anger for her own stupidity in picking such an ill-suited partner. But she was young, only twenty-one when they met, and so she was somewhat forgiving of herself as well. She seemed eager to talk, and I was happy to listen. Sarah seemed like a kind, caring, giving person, so I didn't feel put off listening. If anything, I was happy to do it as she seemed like a fine person.

That night, Sarah made hamburger helper for dinner, and after she read a bedtime story to Lucy, she came out of Lucy's room into the living room where I was watching a Mariner baseball game and smoking a Viceroy. She sat down on the couch, and asked if I want anything to drink, like wine or beer, or if I wanted a little pot. I opt for the pot, as it had the greatest potential for relaxation and I haven't had any in a while. Lately, my luck with pot had been good. No bad trips. Sarah said she smoked every night after she put Lucy to bed. We passed the rather mild Mexican pot back and forth. It was nice. She was nice. I could see that Sarah was in need of male attention, and I found her sweet and warm. I was sort of attracted to her, more as a person than physically, but physically attracted enough. After we smoked the j, moments pass with the both of us quiet as Stevie Wonder's "Talking Book" played on the turntable. Then, I thought to myself, fuck it, and made a move towards Sarah. After all, we were both sitting on the couch together, having shared the j, so it was not a stretch to make the physical move. Sarah seemed glad and eager. We fell onto the carpeted floor for a while in make-out mode. Then, Sarah whispered, "Do you want to go into my bed?" The answer, of course, was yes, which I expressed with a nod and an "Uh huh." We walked hand in hand into her room and the rest was history.

We spent the next two days together. Sarah showed me the sights of Seattle, including Pike's Place, and various places of physical, historical or cultural interest. She was knowledgeable and low key, if somewhat plump. By day three, with this suddenly thrust upon domestic bliss, I became increasingly restless. Sarah was a lovely person, but she was not my endpoint. Time to head down the coast and meet my destination. Enough traveling. As they said in Yiddish, shen genug. Enough already.

The next morning I hit Highway 101, and soon I was at the border of Oregon and Washington. Another few hours and I arrived in Mendocino, California around 7 pm, wiped out and hungry. I stopped at the Mendocino Cafe and ordered a burger, fries, and a coke, my go to meal. Well, what the fuck. I was 23, 5'10.5", and 148 lbs. I could handle the calories. Metabolism of a hummingbird. Now, I had to find a place to crash. Hitting a local bar, I ran into some really weird hippie types, maybe the weirdest yet. A guy who calls himself Dancer was quite stoned, though drinking beer as well. We got into the usual conversation, where I was going, where I'd been, what was I into, what kind of drugs did I have, would I like to get stoned. On this night, Dancer told me most travelers crashed on the beach. The waves were awesome and the beach was pretty soft, sand-wise that was. He offered me some pot, but I passed and headed to the Mendo beach. I pulled my car off to the side just before it got pitch black. I laid my sleeping bag down, got out my flashlight and my paperback, "The Family" by Ed Sanders, a former member of the Fugs, the most authentic version of the story of Charlie Manson. I was on a California kick, wanting to read everything I could get my hands on about California, especially the contemporary scene. I had read "Making of a Counterculture," about the intellectual influences on the counter-cultural scene: Ginsberg, Leary, Watts, Paul Goodman, Marcuse, Norman O. Brown, and Fritz Perls. The book covered a wide spread, from psychedelic drugs. to Eastern mysticism, left wing politics, new wave style and the human potential movement. I had read some Kerouac as well: "On the Road," "Dharma Bums," specifically about Berkeley and the poet Gary Snyder, circa 1955, and lastly, "Big Sur," about Kerouac's alcoholic, speed-fueled hallucinogenic blow out at Ferlinghetti's cabin down in Big Sur while he was trying to write, and get away from the crowds after becoming a celebrity.

The Ed Sanders book about Chuck Manson scared the shit out of me. What was I getting myself into? People out here were fucking nuts. And not all the fun kind of nuts. Some, the dangerous kind. Like Chuck. But I was drawn, and had been since the earliest days with the Mouseketeers in the late fifties, through the Beach Boy thing of the early sixties, and then into the Free Speech Movement of 1964 at Berkeley, and the anti-war movement, which also began in Berkeley, and of course the hippie movement in the Haight. I guess I was scared, but ultimately undaunted by the horrors depicted in the Charlie Manson book. I was going. I was primed. I was ready. Too late to turn back now. One night before I hit Berkeley. Dancer and his weird soundtrack notwithstanding. Fucking Dancer had asked me if I was into the soundtrack. I said yes, but I didn't really know what he was referring to, other than some strange cosmic vibration, present if you paid attention when things went quiet, particularly outside near the ocean. He said you could hear it. Sort of like a presence, but coming from nature. In my sleeping bag, and not stoned, I actually tried to listen for it, and thought I could detect a swooshing sound. Maybe that was it, maybe that was the voice of god. Actually, it wasn't til later that I was told that it was the sound emanating from my eardrum, indicating, perhaps, early signs of tinnitus. But I was too ignorant to sort that out, and believe it or not, despite my New York cynicism, on some minimal level, I was susceptible to countercultural gobbledygook, or maybe I just wanted to believe. Ed Sanders and I lasted about twenty minutes before I fell sound asleep, only to awaken eight hours later with the sun rising at 6:20. I headed back to the cafe, which opened at 7, for coffee and bacon and eggs. My money stash was holding. I started at around $2500, and had about $1000 left. Time to head out on the highway.

"On my way to sunny California, on my way to spend another sunny day. Water, water, get yourself in the clear cool water."

I loved the Beach Boys' California Saga, from Holland, newly released two weeks before I left NYC, and an album which I was on like stink on shit. Four hours down Highway 1 into Sonoma County, then Gualala and Jenner Beach, down past Point Reyes into Marin County. It wouldn't be long now. About an hour. Past Olema, into San Rafael, then onto the Richmond/San Rafael Bridge, I got onto Highway 580 and then 80, El Cerrito, Albany. The sign up ahead said Gilman Street, Berkeley. And then my exit. University Avenue-UC Berkeley. Turning right off the exit, I did a circular turn onto University, and I was fucking here. At last. Yee-ha. I had an address, too. My main man Cal Zamansky from OSU days was living on Walnut Street near campus. I parked my car, hiked up the three flights of stairs, and knock on old Cal's door a number of times. Finally, Doug from the apartment down the hall came out. He said, "If you're looking for Cal, he's at work delivering mail. But I'm his friend and you can hang out with me while you wait."

I immediately discovered he was another OSU Refugee who had been living out here for about a year. His name was Doug Billips, and he lived with his wife Irene. He offered me something to drink and some pot, both of which I accepted. Next thing I knew, Doug and his wife Irene and I were on his carpet listening to Stevie Wonder's "Inner Visions," a mellow, melodic, and rhythmic album. This went on for a couple of hours until Doug heard the sounds of footsteps.

"It must be Cal," Doug said.

We got up in unison and intercepted Cal before he went into his apartment. Cal was taken aback, but not completely surprised. He knew I was coming out, but he didn't know exactly when. He changed out of his postman uniform and came into Doug's, where he proceeded to get lit as well. It was opening night in Berkeley, California, my new home.

It was immediately clear that I would not be able to crash indefinitely with these newfound old and new friends. It wouldn't be right or fair, so the very next day I went to the local city housing area, also known as the Berkeley Co-Op.

CHAPTER 5

The Promised Land (June-October 1973)

This community owned grocery store was where the local youth and twenty-somethings searched for housing and roommates on the co-op bulletin board. My idea was to find a whole house first, and then look for roommates. That way, I became the holder of the lease, and could exert purging power if push came to shove. I found a place in South Berkeley, A five-bedroom house for $400. Now all I had to do was find roommates to fill up the other four rooms. I gave the landlord the first, last, and cleaning deposit, totaling $1000. Then I proceeded to go looking for roommates. This too I accomplished by answering ads on the co-op bulletin board. I found two roommates in a hurry. One was a recent Cal grad in Sociology from Hermosa Beach named Steve, another Steve, who would, in the not-too-distant future, be called Bugsy. The other was a blonde, waiflike, street urchin named Sky, who had run away from central California. She was 17. Move in date was June 30, 1973. We all agreed to move in that night. Furnitureless. With minimal bedding, a few chairs, and some blankets, we jointly made a food shop. Steve made a casual suggestion.

"Why not drop some acid in celebration of inauguration night at our new place on Atherton Street?"

He had come upon some windowpane acid. There seemed to be a lot of it going around. We agreed with strangely minimal trepidation. This was acid, after all. But what the hell. At the onset of darkness, we dropped. Three strangers, exploring a new domicile, tripping, hallucinating our brains out. Roommates turning into imaginary beasts, wild animals one moment and back to human form the next. Each bare room like an uncharted continent, the crevices, walls, and cornices taking on their own uniqueness and singular beauty. Eight hours of this topsy turvy visual and mental intensity and we were all spent. We went to sleep around 6 am. I woke up at noon on Sunday morning. I was wiped out, depleted, molecules reorganized, revamped. Cleansed. A new me. Or at least the feeling of a new me. I was not sure I know the difference, or cared. It felt like a mental vacuum cleaning, a fresh start, with all the detritus cleared out, synapses pruned and wires strengthened. I was ready to go, but needed a day off for my wiped-out body to catch up with my newly refreshed and recharged brain. The day was spent in a more or less vegetative state. I picked up "The Electric Kool Aid Acid Test" by Tom Wolfe. The paperback was perfect, as it dealt authoritatively with the subjective feeling of being on acid, not to mention the rundown on hip life in the Bay Area in the sixties, which I had sadly missed. I was always feeling as if things going on in New York were not as cool, or even close to how progressive, adventurous, and brave the scene was on the west coast, particularly in San Francisco and Berkeley. My desire to be on the hippest cutting edge of what was going on in the culture was only matched by some latent fear, reinforced by my previous psychotic episodes, of going too far and straying from the edges of the straight world or respectability. I guess I wanted both. To be the most rebellious on the one hand, while at the same time, despite all protestations to the contrary, some recognition (approval) by official channels (Dad) and all the other symbolic representations of established authority. This was my primordial and never changing conflict. The desire to say, "Fuck you," to Dad, establishments, and what was socially appropriate, with all the rage that I could bring to it, and yet, on the other hand, to gain their assent. Because a part of me did want the approval of the authorities. I hated that part, and tried to pretend it didn't exist a lot of the time, and yet it was the part that held me back from going all in on the countercultural thing, the part of me that was also critical of the countercultural thing, of the people who seemed too kneejerk. Too reactive, engaging in rebellion for the hell of it. Of course, part of the rebellion did have some substance. The establishment was fucked. Racist, anti-women, anti-anything for ones that didn't conform to some myth of appropriateness, niceness. I was just another Holden Caulfield, another Sal Paradise from the imagination of Jack Kerouac. But I was also authentically caught up in the whirlwind of the times.

I spent the next day at Doug and Irene's apartment, allowing my body to rest up from the previous night's psychedelic pummeling. And then, I returned to my new place with my new roommates, two people and two rooms short. The next new guy, soon to be a law student at Boalt Hall, the UC Berkeley law school, was named Earl, a Vietnam vet, but now staunchly anti-war. Earl was clearly bright and funny. Sky, Steve, and I quickly caucused, and Earl was in. One more to go. The last roommate would prove to be the kicker, as over the next couple of months, we went through a couple of flameouts. I got conned into taking a couple who turned out to be junkies. I shoulda known better as one of the guy's names was Pleasure. He was named

Pleasure because he gave pleasure to people, according to his inane girlfriend Honey, a piece of work in her own right. What assholes. Pleasure and his junkie girlfriend lasted four weeks before we got rid of them. Luckily, I had purging powers. Finally, in late August, after almost two months of riff raff, we settled upon a young woman and her dog. Carrie, the woman, and Treeka, her dog, a Golden Retriever, were sweet as sugar. Now we were five, but not through with the configuration, as Sky, the runaway child from Central Valley, was apparently not through with her running ways. She took off about a month into her stay on Atherton Street, leaving us one roommate behind again. But not to worry, almost immediately we filled her slot with Rosmary, a soon to be senior in environmental studies, also at Cal. Now we were at five, and would stay that way for the next ten months. Rosmary, Carrie, Earl , Steve, and me, the leaseholder.

Berkeley was sort of transitioning. Still heavily ensconced in the 60's ethos of anti-war, civil rights, and Black power, and now adding a strong current emphasis on feminism, gay liberation, and environmentalism. The place had the feel of a scene where you could do anything you pleased, as long as you didn't hurt anyone. A dominant hippie vibe proliferated. That first month, I still had some money left from my New York savings, but it was going fast, and I would definitely have to get a printing job within the month.

There was one thing I had promised myself upon leaving New York, and that was to find a regular softball game. This came to fruition rather fast. One day while I was walking around Sproul Plaza on the UC Berkeley campus, I ran into an old New Rochelle, University of Wisconsin friend, who was living in Berkeley, Jon Terner. Turns out, he knew of a game on the UC campus. He introduced me to his friend Sol, one of the mainstays of the game. Sol, a grad student in sociology, and a rather affable fellow, informed me about Dewey and Donn, the founders of the game, which was now into its 6th year. They told me to show up at Sproul Hall, the site of the girls' gym and softball field, that Saturday. If I showed up on time, I'd get in. In other words, a choose up game. Sure enough, that next Saturday, I showed up at eleven, right on time, on the 14th of July. I was the tenth person to show, and I got to play. The game was full of colorful characters. In addition to Sol, a colorful character in his own right, there was the Statman, whose nickname was self-evident, Holden, an army vet and proto fascist, Dewey, the founder, Victor, the world's greatest frisbee player, and Mike Deldebbio, Vietnam vet, PTSD sufferer, and borderline psychotic. Plus, there were a myriad of others who would be passing through, and who still pass through fifty-two years later as I still participate. Back then, the game was weed infested. David, the Statman, provided the weed, which was quite strong by the standards of the day. Usually Hawaiian (Maui Wowie) or Columbian (Lumbo), the effects could be felt by the 4th inning, when the game would invariably slow down, pace and perception wise. Another highlight was the presence of the UC women, who in those days were known to nude sunbathe on the balcony, which also functioned as the right field bleachers for our game. The bleachers became a popular spot for all hitters due to the dispersal effect the ball had on the sunbathers. Lefty and righty hitters would get up and try to reach the bleachers in order to create mayhem, hence garnering the ball players a gander at the naked breasts of the undergraduates. In these heavy-duty feminist days in Berkeley, the men of the town had to keep their lustful ways on the downlow. It was then that the "sensitive male" was in its nascence. The Berkeley men had to pretend to be emotional and sensitive, all the while ogling the beauties sauntering by. A code word was established for these occasions to maintain this sensitive male persona. "Major league scout" became the chant to signal players whenever a good looking girl would come walking by, bringing the game to a momentarily halt. Another feature of the game was anonymity. It was as if the game was a self-enclosed universe, in that none of the players knew or inquired about any of the other players, as to what they did, or what they believed. All questions and statements were focused strictly on the game itself, thus affording the players a respite from the ongoing pressures of status, money, and career that were inevitably present for most of us, all in our twenties or early thirties. The game itself was of fairly good quality. Many of the players had played on their high school teams, some on their college teams, and, on rare occasions, an ex-minor leaguer would show up. There was a lot of arguing over calls, rules violations, and changing of calls, but the vibes never got to the point where actual fisticuffs broke out. The venom stayed on a verbal level. There was plenty of shouting, but no pushing, shoving, kicking or punching. The game would afford me a structure, both then, and to this day. I could rely on softball from 11-3 pm Saturday and Sunday from April – November, or when the rains came. In northern California, there are only two seasons: wet and dry. Wet was November to April, and dry was the rest of the months. Structure was a good thing. Whether I was working or not, softball was my one enduring structure of the next 50+ years. Life in Berkeley was beginning to take shape. Roommates, check. Friends, check. Softball, check.

Now I needed two other elements and all would be set: a job and a girlfriend. I did have a trade to fall back on - printing. And I did have a girl – Carole - but she was back in Columbus, not a practical arrangement by any stretch. By the end of July, it was time to look for work. The woman situation would work itself out. My first move, job-wise, was to contact the local printing press union, and apply for work. They had something for me right away. A gig in San Francisco, union scale, would pay well, but unfortunately the press I was expected to run was over my head. It was a two colored machine, and I had been trained in one color on a smaller machine. My ineptitude became apparent almost instantly, and after two days I was let go. But a few weeks after, I got picked up for a job on a feeder machine that printed sheets of labels and supplied varnish for canned goods. The job was located in San Jose, a one-hour commute, and again, a union job. This one was within my skill range, but tough to get there on time. I had to be at work by 7am. I was up by 5, and out the door by no later than 6. I was frequently late, and quickly put on notice that my behavior would not be tolerated. Clearly, this was a struggle. Usually the shifts were 7-5. But sometimes, the shifts were 5am to 3pm. It was brutal getting up. One time, I got home from a 5-3 shift, and I decided to take a bath, but I was so tired that I fell asleep in the bathtub, sliding down into the water and nearly drowning, waking up just in time before I went under for good. The job itself was both monotonous and dangerous. I was positioned at the end of a varnish press, where huge sheets of labels would go through a conveyor belt, automatically applying varnish. My job was to catch the sheets at the end and put them atop a wooden box, arranging the sheets neatly. I wore gloves, but the biggest hazard was the ongoing breathing in of the varnish all day, every day, leaving me with the spins by the end of my shift. The work was fucked up, and couldn't be good for my brain cells. Luckily, the spinning diminished by the time I got into my car to go home. My usual thought at the end of shifts was, "This job sucks. I fucking hate this fucking job." But it paid $5.90 per hour plus time and a half for overtime. The job lasted about six weeks, until I got fired for my third lateness. My reaction was mixed. I was glad to not have to make the commute to San Jose anymore, or endure the varnish fumes, or the ordeal of the alienation that came from the monotony of the job. But I was sort of depressed about being fired from my second job in three months. This time I would be eligible for unemployment insurance, and I had amassed a nice sum of money in a short period of time, which I hadn't had time to spend due to the long hours of work during the previous six weeks.

By October, softball season was over. The rains had come. I was out of work again, but I had some extra money. What was I gonna do? I found myself thinking about Carole and decided to call her, to tell her about Berkeley, and to once again try to persuade her to come out west to be with me. But once again, she was adamant about staying in Columbus. She was still eager to lay down roots, settle down, marry, and have kids, the full catastrophe, and still wanting to do it with me, but not in Berkeley. Of course, my need for adventure and really liking it here in Berkeley couldn't allow me to go back, despite how much I felt that she was the rightest person for me I had ever known. Despite how well we got along, how well we understood each other, despite how dedicated and devoted we had been to each other, despite all that good stuff, all the phone call with Carole did was make me feel it was not to be. I was not ready to give up trying, but we both knew that each of us needed to lead our own lives for the time being. Maybe forever. It was still up in the air. But neither of us was willing to give up trying, not just yet. We agreed to continue speaking monthly, a promise we both kept, and we both tried to initiate. The phone call was a bummer, for sure. I needed to get away, and I had extra dough in my pocket. My first thought was Vegas. Too far. Second thought: Reno. Closer. By myself.

My roommates were either working or in school, so I went to play the craps tables. This was a return to gambling for the first time since going to the track the night before I left for college almost five years previously. I grabbed my stash of money, got into my Red Octopus, and headed out on Highway 80 East to the Sierras for fun, adventure, excitement, and the unknown. A three and a half hour drive.

I listen to the FM radio, underground rock station KSAN for the first hour or so and then uncharacteristically turn it off, driving in silence. My mind, the part not focused on driving, immediately goes to fantasizing about what the casino in Reno will be like. I've never been inside one, only seen what they look like on tv and in the movies. That's all I've got to go on, but those fantasies quickly shift into the nature of risk, gambling, CHANCE and LUCK itself. Not even thinking about gambling, my mind wanders into the role chance and luck play in life, in my life. I start doing a series of what if's. What if Carole changes her mind and comes to live with me? What if my mother hadn't died, what would my life be like? What if Marla and I hadn't broken up and gotten married? That's what if I've contemplated a lot and concluded it wouldn't work at all. But yet it comes up on my mental rolodex. I think about her too damn much, I say. But the mental wondering moves on. Now the big one. What if I hadn't had my psychotic episode when I was eighteen? What would my life be like? Less pain and suffering, I think, but in the next instant, maybe my life would be less interesting. Now the movie "It's a Wonderful Life" the 40's classic pops up. The movie where, in a climactic moment, Jimmy Stewart in despair wonders what life would have been like if he had never been born. I flash on that for a second. I like life too much to entertain that fantasy, so quickly move on. Events, momentary decisions, some thought out, some not, by me and by others important to me. It all seems so random. Chance, luck. At that moment I think I didn't have a lot to say about the way my life went. Maybe that's true for everybody. Luck and chance. We tell ourselves we make choices, but do we? We need to believe it, I tell myself, suddenly pulling out of my temporary trance and remembering that I'm driving. You damn well better think you make choices, are in control. Remember, it was you who decided to drive up to Reno. To play the crap tables. Where the roll of the dice is everything. The roll of the dice. Maybe that's all that life is. A roll of the dice. I quickly disabuse myself of this notion and drive on. Too scary. Maybe too real.

The End.

www.ingramcontent.com/pod-product-compliance
Lightning Source LLC
Chambersburg PA
CBHW060410310726
48976CB00003B/1006